MW00929755

The King's Magic

Book One
of the
Chronicles of Nèra Toli

THE KING'S MAGIC

BOOK ONE

OF THE

CHRONICLES OF NÈRA TOLI

Written and Illustrated by

F. G. WILLIAMS

NÈRA TOLI PRESS

SAN DIEGO

The King's Magic: Book One of the Chronicles of Nėra Toli
Copyright © 2014 by F. G. Williams
All rights reserved under International and Pan-American
Copyright Conventions.
Published in the United States of America by Nėra Toli Press.

First edition by Nėra Toli Press, USA, 2014

Requests for information should be addressed to:
Nėra Toli Press
P.O. Box 503465
San Diego, CA 92150-3465

ISBN: 978-0-9839064-1-4 (b&w pb)
ISBN: 978-0-9839064-4-5 (color pb)
ISBN: 978-0-9839064-2-1 (e-book)

Special Editions:
ISBN: 978-0-9839064-3-8 (color hc)
ISBN: 978-0-9839064-0-7 (b&w hc)

http://thekingsmagic.com
http://neratolipress.com

for my husband and daughters

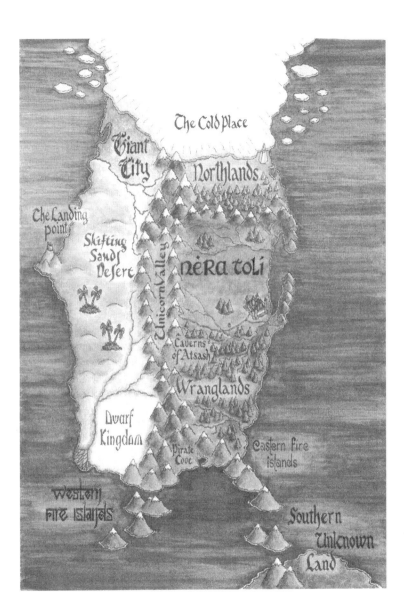

The Cold Place

Giant City

Northlands

The Landing Point

Skifting Sands Desert

Unicorn Valley

nera toli

Caverns of Atsash

Wranglands

Dwarf Kingdom

Pirate Cove

Eastern Fire Islands

Western Fire Islands

Southern Unknown Land

Contents

Chapter I
UNEXPECTED NEWS

Ꞓꞏꞑꞑ꞉ꞑꞑꞒꞏ (decorative script)

"Luke! Lexi!" a voice echoed. "Your breakfast is getting cold!"

At the opposite end of the castle, two children lounged on the roof of the east tower. The prince and princess smiled mischievously at each other, perched above the sea of mist. They watched the sun emerge above the fog, bathing them in its warm, orange glow.

"I'm famished!" Luke declared, his stomach growling through his pajamas. "I wish we could have breakfast right here." The sun lit up his freckled face and his sandy, uncombed curls.

1

"No one is bringing our breakfast all the way up here," laughed Lexi. "If they did, they would find out that this is our secret spot. Let's head down." The princess edged her way off the roof, swinging down through the tower window.

Luke shimmied down behind his twin sister. As he neared the edge, his foot slipped on some loose shingles. In an instant, he was flying through the air.

As he fell, time itself seemed to slow to a halt. He waited to splash into the filthy moat below, but instead slammed against the castle wall. Luke looked up to see his sister clutching his outstretched arm.

"Watch those loose shingles, would you?" Lexi said as she pulled her brother up. Despite Lexi's calm voice, Luke knew that she was just as shaken as he was. Both children laughed nervously.

"If I were Mom, I would yell at you right now for being so careless," Lexi finally snapped.

"If you were Mom, you would yell at me for breaking a hundred different rules this morning and for being up here in the first place," Luke grinned.

"I am glad no one knows about our secret place, especially not *her*," Lexi laughed, hauling her brother through the window.

"Luke! Lexi! Your *breakfast!*"

As they made their way down the spiral staircase, the woman's shouts drifted up like smoke. It was only Nana, their nurse.

To a stranger, she might sound stern, but the prince and princess knew otherwise. Nana was as indulgent as their mother was strict. The twins laughed as they descended into the mist-covered castle below.

A few secret shortcuts later, they appeared in the royal dining hall. The long table was completely empty except for two stone cold bowls of porridge. The twins sat and ate, feeling sorry for themselves for not getting chocolates for breakfast like princes and princesses in other kingdoms.

* * *

On their way back to their chambers, whom should the twins meet but their mother, Queen Tabitha, alongside creepy Count Damien! The queen smiled broadly, but her eyes had a glassy quality to them.

"Good morning, Mother," the twins chorused politely. Luke bowed automatically. As she curtseyed, Lexi wondered absently what their mother would do if they tried to hug her. So elegant and beautiful, the queen seemed oddly untouchable.

How long had Queen Tabitha been so distant? It had not always been this way. Ever since Count Damien had come to court, their parents—and especially their mother—had not been their normal selves.

"Good morning, children," the queen said mechanically.

"You will meet your new tutor in an hour," Count Damien smirked.

"What happened to Timothy?" Luke blurted. Since Luke and Lexi had begun their schooling, they had been taught by an ancient and illustrious scholar known as Timothy.

Timothy was so old that some doubted he was even mortal. Timothy had served their father, his father before him and even—so it was said—their great-grandfather. For three generations, there had been peace and prosperity in Nėra Toli.

"He has been replaced," said Count Damien sharply. "A younger teacher will better meet your needs. Professor Albert is a very advanced thinker. These are changing times we live in."

"But everything is going well in the kingdom!" Lexi erupted. "How can you send Timothy away after all these years? Why do we have to go and change everything when there aren't even any problems?" Getting rid of Timothy was like packing all things good into a trunk and tossing it into the sea.

"Remember yourself!" the count snapped. "It has been ordered by the king. Period."

Lexi glared at Count Damien. She turned to her mother for help, but the queen's expressionless face frightened her. It was obvious that the queen was unnaturally under Count Damien's influence.

"I would not worry," said the count. "You will not have to endure your new tutor for too long. Your parents and I have just settled the terms of your marriage to Duke Whitmore of the Eastern Fire Islands."

"But I am barely fourteen!" cried Lexi. "Why must you marry me off and be rid of me so soon?"

"By the time your mother was your age she was already married to your father and pregnant with you and your brother," Count Damien retorted. "If you are old enough to bear children, you are old enough to marry."

Lexi bit her tongue, but her face betrayed her rage. Tears appeared in her eyes.

"As for you, Luke," the count added, "we are still negotiating your betrothal to Princess Saskia of the Northlands. It is a good match and will double our territory. She is only seven, so it will be quite a few years until *your* marriage."

Luke reeled in shock. Here he was, engaged to a toddler! He had never met Princess Saskia, but shuddered to remember Duke Whitmore from a banquet the previous year. The duke had lumbered around like a grizzly and had hungrily eyed Lexi. Worse yet, Duke Whitmore was almost as old as their father!

"Well, everything is settled then," said Count Damien. "You will meet your new tutor in an hour. Be at the balcony *on time*. The king will be making a proclamation to the people and introducing Professor Albert."

"Now hurry to your chambers, children," the queen added vacuously.

* * *

Uncharacteristically early, Prince Luke and Princess Lexi waited in the salon by the royal balcony. While there were other balconies, this was where the royal emblem hung. It was here that King Simon addressed his subjects, with the royal family beside him. He said it reassured the people.

Luke and Lexi waited on a red velvet sofa, each dressed in the finest clothes in the kingdom and terrified of wrinkling them. As they sat together, it was striking how different the twins looked from one another. They did not even look like siblings, much less *womb-mates.*

Princess Alexandra, called Lexi for short, had dark features and the olive skin of a field hand. Despite her neatly styled hair and diamond-studded tiara, she had a half-wild look about her. Prince Luke, on the other hand, had sandy curls and fair skin. Only his pale gray eyes hinted at his stubbornness and fiery will.

The twins waited impatiently, feeling restless and uneasy. Their world was suddenly unrecognizable, with their beloved teacher gone and replaced by a stranger. Worse yet was the fact that the course of their lives had just been decided without their consent.

Neither twin had thought much about marriage, that inevitable aspect of royal life. Despite all that Timothy had taught them, he had not mentioned marriage. Lexi wished she could tell Timothy all about her betrothal and get *his* advice.

"I wish Count Damien had never come to court!" Luke said, breaking the silence. "Mother has not been herself since he arrived."

"Who does he think he is?" Lexi vented. "He just shows up and gets himself made advisor. The nerve!"

"I am sure Mom and Dad never would have arranged those matches for us without Count Damien's meddling," said Luke. "I don't understand why Dad even hired him."

"Nana said that Count Damien is supposedly our distant cousin, or something," Lexi suggested. "I bet he just made that up to get Daddy to make him his advisor."

"There is *no* way we are related to Count Damien! He gives me the creeps," Luke spat, "and I bet that new tutor he picked is a real *rezool*."

"Nana said that he only got the job because he is really Count Damien's son."

"*Nephew*," came a voice from behind them. "I am his *nephew*." A tall stranger glowered down at them.

Chapter II
ALBERT'S INTRODUCTION

ꙮꙮꙮꙮꙮꙮꙮꙮꙮꙮꙮꙮ

Luke and Lexi looked up at the towering figure behind them. How long had their new tutor been eavesdropping?

Fortunately, they did not have to stare speechlessly for long. Just then, the king swept into the room, followed by his bustling entourage. Professor Albert's eyes lingered coldly on them as they hurried to greet their father.

"Daddy! Daddy!" they cried, relieved to escape Albert's glare. King Simon's eyes lit up and he embraced his children warmly. His salt-and-pepper beard tickled their faces as he gave each of them a peck on the cheek. Both twins instantly felt safe from their worries about Count Damien and Professor Albert.

"Well," the king said, "I believe we had better say good morning to the all the people who have gotten up early just for us."

Before long, the children stood out on the balcony next to their parents, only half-listening to their father's address. The early morning mist had not quite burned off yet, but sunbeams already lit up the castle courtyard. Lexi's mind wandered as she listened to her father's deep voice.

It was so strange how Count Damien had gotten rid of their old tutor literally overnight. Only the day before, they had sat in the south tower, listening to one of Timothy's long, wandering lectures about astronomy, daffodils and the importance of speaking Dwarfish with the proper accent.

They often had trouble following Timothy's lessons, but loved to poke among his dusty, ancient books and play with the strange contraptions that littered his drafty tower.

Lexi fondly remembered the large painting that hung behind Timothy's immense desk. It was the most incredible, lifelike landscape she had ever seen—depicting a long valley and a distant range of snowcapped mountains. By some marvelous enchantment, the painting appeared to be alive.

Of all the wonders of Timothy's tower, that living painting was her favorite. Lexi often found herself distracted from her schoolwork, staring past

Timothy's desk, captivated by that window into another reality.

Some days, herds of wild unicorns moved across the plains. Other days it poured rain in Timothy's painting. There were even seasons in the picture. Lexi shivered to remember it. Now Timothy was gone and his wonderful room was probably barren. Lexi felt cold and empty.

* * *

"Ouch!" blurted Lexi. Luke had pinched her arm. Their father's speech was over and everyone was going back inside.

"Don't pinch me!" Lexi snapped, kicking her brother in the shin once they were back inside.

"So the future king lets himself be pushed around by a girl," a sinister voice said. It was that awful new tutor, Albert, again.

This time there was no escape—their mother also peered at them, silently ordering them not to move. With one last glance around for her father, Lexi curtseyed at her mother and Albert. Luke stood by her side, his eyes fixed on the strange man.

"Albert, meet my children, Luke and Lexi," the queen said. "Lexi is still learning to behave herself as befits royalty."

"Yes, Mother," said Lexi, her face turning red. "Nice to meet you, Professor Albert, sir."

"Charmed," he replied coolly. "And Prince Luke—how nice to finally meet *you*!"

Prince Luke nodded awkwardly. He knew Professor Albert only fawned because Luke was heir to the throne. The prince could not think of anything civil to say, so he cleared his throat instead. He examined his new tutor skeptically.

Professor Albert had violet eyes that looked even more unnatural paired with his limp, strawberry blond hair. It made Luke's own eyes water just to look at Albert's hairless red-tinged eyelids. What Luke most disliked, however, was the professor's almost imperceptible smirk.

"Well, Mother, is it all right if we get going now?" Luke asked. "Lots of studying to do . . ."

"Fine," the queen said. "You may go."

"Lessons begin at eight o'clock tomorrow morning," Albert added. "Do not make me wait."

* * *

On the way back to their chambers, the prince and princess heard footsteps behind them. They recognized Count Damien and Professor Albert's voices echoing down the corridor toward them. Luke and Lexi looked around the stone hallway for an escape.

The twins ducked behind a familiar tapestry to their right. Safely out of sight, they opened a small wooden door and slipped into the darkness. When Count Damien and Professor Albert strode by moments later, nothing betrayed the twins' recent presence.

Inside the tunnel, Luke lit a torch. Light danced on the stone walls and ceiling. Elsewhere in the castle, the ceilings were so high that light never seemed to reach them. In this little nook, though, the ceilings were comfortably low—just the right size for the prince and princess.

Neither twin knew who had built this network of secret passages. They guessed that the tunnels had probably existed for as long as the castle itself. It had been Timothy who had first shown them these catwalks.

"And to think that these tunnels are good for more than shortcuts and hiding from Nana at bedtime . . ." said Lexi mischievously.

"Professor Albert sure gives me the creeps," Luke whispered, as if still afraid of being heard. "Thank goodness we got away! I would hate to have to talk to him again."

"Let's go down to the kitchen for a snack," Lexi suggested. "That will make us both feel better. Cook always has cookies ready, just for us."

A few minutes later, the twins emerged into the kitchen. In the middle of the room stood a large wooden table, littered with delicacies-in-progress. Copper pots and pans hung from the ceiling, while the huge oven took up an entire wall.

An immense man, dressed all in white, danced around obliviously, while energetically beating a dozen eggs. A redheaded scullery maid giggled as she sat peeling potatoes in the corner: The cook often failed to notice the arrival of the prince and princess.

The cook glanced up and scowled at his assistant, who motioned toward Luke and Lexi. Tossing aside his bowl, the cook bounded over to the royal twins like a mustachioed polar bear. He scooped them up in a hearty, suffocating squeeze.

"My favorite prince and princess!" he laughed. "What can I get for you? Would you like a cake or a pudding, or something heartier—a beef stew, perhaps?"

Luke's eyes lit up and he smiled. "I was thinking of milk and cookies."

"Of course!" the cook laughed. "Some milk and cookies for Your Highness. Why it just so happens that I have a batch that is still warm! And for Your Highness, my Princess?"

"The same, please," Lexi replied. She liked how the cook always had some warm cookies and milk for them, at any time of day. Moreover, he was always kind and in good spirits.

At a little wooden table with two wooden chairs, the prince and princess dipped their rich chocolate chip cookies into oversized mugs of milk. The cook returned to singing and dancing around the kitchen and the potato peeler, her work finished, disappeared. In turn, Luke and Lexi also slipped away, taking a half-dozen cookies with them.

* * *

Back in the secret passageway, Luke removed the torch from its place on the wall. The twins ate while they walked, leaving a trail of crumbs. When they reached a corner where the entire passageway turned left, Luke noticed some light peeking through the stone wall before them.

"What is that?" mumbled Lexi, shoving another cookie into her mouth.

"It looks like a crack in the wall," said Luke. "I thought this was a storage room. There were never any lights in there before."

"Let's take a look. You go first." Lexi pushed her brother toward the peephole.

Luke's eye stayed glued to the crack in the wall, uttering only an occasional "Wow!" Lexi, regretting her caution, peppered him with questions about what he could see.

"Incredible! There's a whole laboratory and everything!" Luke finally said. "I never knew that room was so huge inside. And look at that python!"

"Come on, move over already," said Lexi impatiently. Finally, Luke turned the peephole over to her. Extending out below her was a cross between a dungeon and a library.

There were horrible torture devices and strange beasts in cages. She saw animal and human body parts in apothecary jars. Beakers simmered over candles. A cauldron bubbled over glowing embers in the fireplace. Near the fire lounged a python that was so big it looked like it could eat princes and princesses without a second thought.

Just when Lexi started wondering who owned all this suspicious equipment, Count Damien and Professor Albert burst into the chamber. Lexi jumped and banged into her brother, who hovered behind her.

"Let's get out of here," she urged.

"We have to tell Dad about this," Luke agreed, still dazed. "Those two have got to be up to no good. Why in Nèra Toli would a royal advisor and tutor need potions and torture devices?"

Luke's words echoed in their ears as they hurried to their chambers.

Chapter III
NIGHT FLIGHT

ꜟꞈꝏꞁ ꜟꞈꝏꝏꝏ

Luke and Lexi arrived early for dinner, but did not see their father anywhere. They nervously paced around the great hall. A lone servant eyed them oddly.

"Let's just sit down," Lexi whispered, feeling conspicuous and uncomfortable.

"Okay," Luke replied. They found their usual spots, at the midpoint between each end of the long table, where their mother and father always sat. Lexi tapped nervously on the ornately carved crystal goblet before her.

"Please give it a rest, Sis," said Luke. "You know our glass comes all the way from the Dwarf Kingdom. Father will be cross if you crack another goblet."

"Look! There are a few extra goblets at the table today," Lexi said, pointing. There were two extra place settings at the table—an extra one at each end.

The twins cringed to hear Count Damien and Professor Albert's fawning voices approach. A moment later, the king and queen entered the room, their long robes stretched behind them. The advisor and royal tutor followed, taking their places beside the king and queen. They seemed to enjoy the luxury of the procession a little too much.

Luke and Lexi watched in shocked silence. In the past, the king and queen had only ever occupied the head and foot of the table alone. What was Professor Albert doing next to their father, and Count Damien next to their mother? Luke wanted to speak up, but his voice caught in his throat. No one seemed to notice him.

Dinner proceeded lavishly, with more dishes than the twins could count. The cook had been busy. Luke was so worried he could hardly eat. He had no specific accusations against Count Damien and Professor Albert. All he had was a sick feeling in his stomach.

Lexi gave her brother a knowing glance. She understood how he felt. What hard evidence did they have? An oversized python was hardly proof of treachery.

Even the formaldehyde-preserved body parts proved nothing. After all, their unfortunate owners *could* have died naturally. With all these thoughts on Luke's mind, his dinner might as well have been sand for all he noticed.

Luke awoke from his brooding to see his parents leaving the table. Count Damien and the Professor followed. Without even saying goodbye, the royal parents and their advisors had left their open-mouthed children still sitting at the giant dining table.

What was going on? Now the twins were really worried. How could they ever get a chance to talk to their parents if that nasty advisor and his toady kept hanging about them? Then it occurred to Luke that perhaps that was exactly their intention.

* * *

Lexi awoke in the dark. Someone was shaking her.

"Enough already!" she snapped groggily. "Who is that, anyway?" With some effort, she could just make out Nana's face in front of her, lit by a lone candle.

"Shhhh!" Nana whispered. "We have to go. Now!"

Crawling from her immense canopy bed, Lexi followed Nana in disbelief. The nightgown-clad princess awkwardly stumbled toward the door, sleepily marveling at Nana's confidence in the blackness.

As her senses sharpened, Lexi gradually realized that she was slinking like a thief through the palace in the dead of night. Something was very wrong.

Soon they were in Luke's room and Lexi still had no idea why. As long as she did not ask what was wrong, maybe she could just go back to bed. Her eyelids kept drooping shut.

Then Luke was awake too, instantly aware that his silence was crucial. Although Luke's presence comforted her, Lexi now knew for sure that she was awake and that this, whatever *this* was, was for real.

Before Nana could lead them back out into the hallway, Lexi tugged on her sleeve. Without uttering a peep, the princess pointed through the tarlike blackness to a large mirror on the far wall.

Neither of them could see either the mirror or its ornate gold frame, but Nana followed when Lexi and Luke walked toward it. As Nana watched, Luke pulled on the mirror's frame.

The whole mirror swung outward from the wall. A cold draft swept over Nana, nearly extinguishing the lonely candle. Squinting, she saw Luke and Lexi step forward into the drafty darkness.

A hand reached back toward the old woman. Without knowing whose it was, she clasped it and stepped forward. They pulled the heavy mirror closed behind them.

"Nana, *what* is going on?" Lexi whispered urgently, still clutching her nurse's large, rough hand. Although the secret passage guarded voices from outside ears, the seriousness of the situation seemed to demand hushed tones.

There was a brief scratching sound and then Luke appeared, holding a glowing torch. Lexi's worried face flickered in the yellow light and her yet unanswered question still hung in the air.

"Lexi, Luke," said Nana gravely. "Your lives are in grave danger. Your father has been murdered this very night. Within a few hours, everyone in the castle will be looking for you."

The prince and princess stood there in the darkness, too stunned to speak. Their eyes opened a little wider and they tried to make sense of what they had just heard.

Lexi felt the cold stone floor through her slippers. It seemed to pull her down, sucking the life from her legs, numbing her. Seeing his sister wobble, Luke took her hand. A cold draft whistled through the tunnel and all three shivered.

"Last night at dinner, *you* poisoned your father," Nana told Luke. "By sunrise, no place in this castle will be safe, not even this little nook."

"What are you talking about?" Luke blurted out, his voice echoing down the passage. "I love my father! I would never do anything to hurt him!"

"I know that and you know that," Nana replied, "but when your mother tells the townspeople about how you threatened him at dinner, it will all make so much sense. And when vials of poison are found in Lexi's room, it will be obvious that it was a conspiracy."

"But Nana!" Lexi interjected. "Luke would never threaten Father, much less *kill* him! What are we going to do? Who could do such a thing? Why?"

Before Lexi had even finished speaking, she knew the answer.

"It does not matter who or why, only that you have to get out of here. Tonight. At this very moment. By morning it will be too late. Which way to the stables?" Nana asked, looking right and left down the stone passage.

Soon the royal children and old woman were running past the kitchen. Lexi wished silently that she had saved some of those wonderful cookies. Her stomach growled in agreement.

Then Luke opened a small square door, and all thoughts of cookies were replaced by the overwhelming smell of manure.

Crawling out of a small opening in the wall, they entered the courtyard and hid behind a cart of fertilizer. It took a few minutes for their eyes to adjust to the moonlight. Compared to the total darkness of the secret passageway, the moon's silvery blue glow was blindingly bright.

Quickly getting her bearings, Nana led the twins along the wall to the stable doors and inside. There they saw all the royal steeds. The horses' very breaths seemed loud next to their own soundless steps.

At the far end of the stalls, Luke saw an old, dilapidated wagon. Moonbeams shone through an open window on the wagon's cargo of barrels— apple barrels, by their overripe smell.

Normally, the smell of apples meant that Cook was going to make a delicious apple pie. *How far away all of that is now!* thought Luke.

"These barrels are your only way out of the castle," said Nana. "By the time the castle gates open in the morning, every guard will be looking for you."

Luke and Lexi listened, transfixed.

"The driver of this cart will take you to my son, Evan, who is a tavern keeper. He will help you to safety," continued Nana. "I wish I could offer you more, but here are some sandwiches and a change of clothes."

Nana handed a small knapsack to Lexi, who clutched it as if it contained priceless gems. She and Luke climbed up onto the wagon and bravely squeezed themselves into the open barrels.

Nana pounded the wooden lids shut as quietly as she could, as twenty puzzled horses looked on. Before she stole away, Nana whispered at the pile of barrels that she loved them, not to worry, and that everything would be all right.

Lexi tried not to panic in the close confines of her barrel. In between claustrophobic thoughts, she felt her eyes grow heavier.

What if Nana had killed Father and was now going to kill them? she wondered. *No, it had to be Count Damien or the Professor—after all, they were so creepy. But how did Nana know about all this if she was innocent?*

Lexi's thoughts soon melted away with the smell of hay and apples. Before long, her dreams found her back in the kitchen eating cookies with her brother.

Her brother, on the other hand, listened to his pounding heart for what felt like hours before finally nodding off.

CHAPTER **IV**
THE COUNT'S ANNOUNCEMENT

Luke awoke with a jerk, hitting his head hard. He blinked but could see nothing, not even his own hands. He tried to remember where he was and how he had gotten there. His head throbbed. Finally, memories of the previous night came flooding back to him.

As long as some part of him thought he was only dreaming, the gravity of his situation had escaped him. While half-asleep, he had followed Nana without question or surprise.

Now that he was fully awake, Luke felt a sudden surge of terror that he might suffocate or starve to death. Lexi had all the sandwiches and his stomach growled loudly.

He was starting to hyperventilate when he noticed a patch of light streaming into his barrel. Forgetting his panic, Luke put his eye to the knothole and looked outside.

It must still be early, he thought, noticing that the high castle walls still hid the sun. The wagon stood outside the stables, now hitched to a very large and impatient horse.

Outside in the courtyard, chickens clucked and dogs barked, as if it were any ordinary morning. Horses neighed and boots stomped back and forth past the wagon.

Despite all the normal morning sounds, Luke had a nagging feeling that there was something missing, something different. Then it dawned on him: There were no children laughing or shouting or skipping through the dusty streets.

Even grownups sounded different. The familiar, lighthearted gossip had been replaced by worried whispers. The courtyard seemed somber. Nervous electricity crackled through the cool morning air.

"People of Nèra Toli!" a voice boomed from above. "Gather around." A murmuring grew out of nowhere, as the townspeople seemed to awaken from a trance. The voice continued, "I would appreciate your attention."

Luke could not see the royal balcony from his barrel, but he recognized the deep, daunting voice of Count Damien.

"I am afraid the rumors are true," Count Damien said solemnly. "King Simon has indeed been assassinated. Poisoned, it appears. The evidence points to the prince and princess."

At this, the murmuring grew louder, until the count menacingly cleared his throat.

"The prince was heard yesterday evening threatening the king, telling him to watch his back," he said. "It seems that the princess, doubtless seeking a share of the spoils, engineered the plot. An assortment of poisons was found in her room, identical to those used to murder the king."

"People of Nėra Toli, I can assure you that none mourn the passing of King Simon more than I," Count Damien said. "It pains me that Good Queen Tabitha has been widowed in so vile a manner, betrayed by her own children.

"Yet I rejoice that I may still bring the queen some measure of happiness. One week from this foul murder, she and I will marry. I am honored to succeed such a great ruler as King Simon."

Luke lurched. Nearly choking on his rage, he suddenly found himself sobbing. He felt so angry, but realized that he could do nothing. Even if he burst out of the barrel and proclaimed the truth to the citizens of Nėra Toli, what good would it do?

He would just be arrested and tossed down into the dungeon to rot or await execution. His father was dead and all he could do was to huddle in a barrel reeking of overripe apples. Luke fumed at the idea of seeing his mother marry that scoundrel of a count.

"Hey you in there!" whispered an unfamiliar voice. "Could you be a little quieter? Apples don't normally move around much. We'll get the two of you out of here as soon as that windbag finishes his speech."

Every ounce of hope still left in Luke's heart grabbed hold of this gruff stranger's words. He was not entirely friendless, he reminded himself, quieting his angry sobs. He and his sister would escape from Count Damien's clutches. Then they would avenge their father's murder. The prince clenched his fist.

Luke could not see the kind stranger who spoke to him. He had no idea that his only hope of escape depended on an awkwardly proportioned, disheveled man whom trouble followed wherever he went.

People in the streets smiled at the stocky man who leaned against the barrel-filled wagon. Their expectant glances waited for him to do something foolish at any given moment. While the count droned on, people snuck glances at Luke's benefactor, impatient for him to amuse them.

"And may I remind you, my good subjects, of your duty to cooperate in this matter," boomed Damien's voice.

"I will richly reward anyone who informs me where the prince and princess are. However, those who are uncooperative will face the penalty for treason—*death!* That is all."

Right then, Luke and Lexi's rotund rescuer slipped and fell in the mud. John Boy, as he was known, sat there puzzled for a moment before getting to his feet.

He had not realized how slippery the mud could be right next to the water trough. The townspeople laughed derisively under their breath. John Boy blushed in frustrated embarrassment.

It's just as well that they laugh, John Boy thought. They would never suspect that he was smuggling the prince and princess out of the castle. They thought that he was a bumbling fool, but he was doing something important. Some day they would give him the respect he deserved.

John Boy untied his golden horse from the hitch by the water trough. He took his seat on the bench in front of the wagon and signaled for the equine goliath to move. Nothing. Even the horse failed to take him seriously.

"Depper," he entreated, shaking the reins. "Come on, girl!"

Depper seemed to wait a few extra seconds before moving, as if to say that she was going because she wanted to, instead of out of obedience.

John Boy drove the wagon to the castle gates and waited in line to pass through. The guards were searching people as they left, trying to prevent Luke and Lexi from escaping.

They have no reason to suspect me, John Boy reassured himself. His thinning black hair and his leathery skin testified to his forty uneventful years. *Everyone knows I'm harmless.* He tried hard to look unremarkable.

For all his effort, he only wound up looking that much stiffer and more awkward. He gripped the reins in his shaking, sweaty palms.

"Morning, John Boy!" a guard greeted John Boy. "You don't mind if we take a look at what's in your wagon, do you? It's orders, you know." The guard grinned broadly, exposing his decaying smile.

Both guards made a show of poking around under a few barrels and checking the bench beside John Boy. Despite being dressed for battle, the knights looked relieved at failing to find anything suspicious. They enjoyed wearing armor, but disliked the idea of needing it.

"Well, everything seems to be in order," one guard said.

John Boy exhaled loudly. He had not realized he had been holding his breath. But instead of letting him pass, the other guard prodded one of the barrels in the wagon with his sword.

"You know, my wife was saying just the other day that she'd like to make a batch of cider, but apples are too expensive this year," the guard said.

"I'm sure John Boy could spare a barrel of apples for your wife's sake. No one would even notice that it was gone," the first knight grinned.

John Boy squirmed awkwardly, understanding that a bribe was expected. If they wanted to, the guards could make his exit a lot more difficult. John Boy stared blankly, completely dumbfounded.

Without waiting for a response, the first guard reached forward to roll a barrel out of the wagon. He gave the barrel a good, hard pull. John

Boy instantly realized that it was the barrel containing Lexi.

"No! Not *that* barrel!" he protested in slow motion, but it was too late.

The guard had given the barrel a hard yank, expecting it to be heavy and cumbersome. Instead, it rolled easily off the wagon and slammed onto the ground.

Amazingly, the barrel remained intact. John Boy sighed in relief. Just then, the barrel's lid fell outward, revealing the curled up form of the princess. For a moment, no one moved.

Chapter V
A WILD RIDE

Before the guards realized what was happening, Lexi slid out of the barrel and was back on her feet. A moment later, they recognized the princess and lunged at her.

"Go, John Boy, Go!" Lexi cried, leaping toward the wagon.

In an instant, John Boy was behind the reins again, ordering the horse to go. For a moment, it looked like Depper had no intention of budging. Then, just as Lexi grasped the edge of the wagon, the mammoth beast lunged forward.

Depper pulled that bouncing wagon harder than she had ever pulled a wagon before. The surrounding townspeople jumped away from the stomping hooves and huge wheels. Lexi gripped the tail end of the wagon for dear life. She knew that falling meant death, whether by breaking her neck or by execution.

"Close the portcullis! Raise the drawbridge!" yelled one of the guards. "Don't let them get away!"

The wagon passed through the gate, narrowly avoiding the falling iron bars. The portcullis came within an inch of taking off Lexi's foot, as she was dragged along behind. The drawbridge started lifting as they crossed it, but they plowed onward anyway.

As the great horse leaped through space, John Boy, Luke and Lexi all felt certain that they would never clear the moat. Somehow, in midair, Lexi pulled herself onto the wagon.

For one very long moment, the barrels were weightless. Suddenly, with a hard thump, the wagon hit the ground. They were on the other side of the moat. Depper continued trotting, but slower than before. They were safe.

Just then, several arrows buzzed through the air and hit the back of the wagon. "They are shooting at us!" cried Lexi. "We have to go faster!"

Still excited from the chase, John Boy quickly realized that they had to get off the road. Soon there would be horsemen chasing them down. No matter how fast they went, their pursuers would go faster.

To the right of the highway, John Boy saw endless fields of grain. The wheat and corn blew hypnotically in the wind. *We could hide in the fields,* John Boy thought. No, it would be impossible to hide the wagon. Moreover, driving into the fields would crush the crop and leave an obvious trail. John Boy looked to his left.

On the other side of the road, he could see no more than a few feet. Trees and bushes grew densely, crowding out all light. John Boy shivered. Every child grew up being warned to stay out of the Wranglands, the vast southern forest. Everyone knew that the faeries would steal any child that wandered onto their land. Even grown men feared to step foot in the forest.

John Boy had no desire to find out if the stories were really true. *Still,* he thought, *farmers let their hogs roam through the forest all summer and they seem none the worse for it.*

Besides, he added, trying to convince himself, *if we stay out here on the highway, Count Damien's henchmen will catch us and we'll be dead for sure.*

John Boy took a breath. Depper trotted onward, little knowing her master's mind. John Boy knew that for his idea to work, he would have to move quickly. In an instant, he had jerked the reins. Depper, caught off guard, obeyed him before thinking.

Realizing she had been tricked, she neighed loudly in protest. She plunged into the thicket, bringing the wagon behind her. In a few seconds, they were surrounded by trees.

Looking back toward the road, John Boy saw the shrubbery return to its old position, covering their path. The plants grew so densely that he could barely see the road.

"Luke! Lexi!" called John Boy. "Are you okay?"

31

Lexi looked bedraggled and dusty, but otherwise unharmed by her bumpy ride in the back of the wagon.

"Let me out!" cried Luke, still inside a barrel. As soon as John Boy pried the barrel's lid off, the disoriented prince crawled to the edge of the wagon and vomited.

A noise echoed in the distance. Everyone paused. Galloping hooves sped past along the road. Apparently, the horsemen had failed to notice the spot where the royal fugitives had gone off the road. A final pair of hooves pounded past and then all was silent. They were safe for the time being.

"I was supposed to take you to your nurse's brother for safety, but now that's out of the question," John Boy said. "I had no idea that Count Damien would be so quick on our heels."

"What do you mean?" Luke demanded, having recovered from his case of wagon-sickness. "If we are not going there, where are we going?"

"Should we just rot here in the forest?" Lexi said sarcastically.

"I just saved your necks back there, in case you didn't notice!" John Boy scolded. "We may yet be able to reach your nurse's brother's house. We just can't go by the road, that's all."

"Sorry . . ." the princess apologized, looking down at her feet.

"I think all this stress is getting to us," Luke explained.

"I understand, kidlets," said John Boy. "Keep your chins up. We'll get through this yet."

Immediate danger having passed, the three fugitives looked around. As their eyes adjusted to the low light, they could see that the surrounding forest was stunningly beautiful. Luke was dumbstruck, while all Lexi could say was "Wow!"

It was the most incredible place any of them had ever seen. There were trees and plants of every variety. Flowers sprouted from every possible nook. From the road, the forest appeared forbidding, but from within its beauty was beyond words.

"We don't have time for sightseeing, you two. This wheel broke when we swerved off the road," John Boy said, motioning toward a splintered wheel. "We have to gather our things and go with Depper."

Neither Luke nor Lexi seemed to hear him. John Boy turned to face them, but they were gone. He started to panic but then saw them. Luke had started climbing a nearby tree. Meanwhile, Lexi gathered tulips and daffodils contentedly.

"Hey, you two!" John Boy shouted. "Fill your pockets and knapsack with apples." He pried open another barrel, sending a mountain of apples spilling down into the wagon.

"Why do we have to weigh ourselves down with apples?" asked Lexi. She bent down to pick some strawberries that carpeted the forest floor. "There seems to be plenty to eat here in the forest."

"Stop!" John Boy ordered.

The startled princess dropped her flowers and berries. She looked up at John Boy in annoyance.

"How do you know if what grows here is safe to eat?" John Boy demanded. "Do you want to fall into some hundred-year sleep on account of enchanted fruit? That's at best.

"At worst, that strawberry there might mean death. Do you think I risked my neck back there just to have you kill yourself now with your foolishness?"

"Okay, okay," Lexi harrumphed, opening up the knapsack to pack apples. Luke swung down from his tree and joined her.

A few minutes later, Luke and Lexi sat astride Depper. John Boy stood beside her, holding her harness. The huge horse took a few steps forward. There was no road, no path, and Depper had no idea where to go.

"It's okay, girl," John Boy said. "Just go forward and we'll find the way."

Depper took a few more uneasy steps forward before stopping again. She nervously stamped in place.

"So . . ." Luke cleared his throat. "What exactly is your plan? You said that it was out of the question for us to get to Nana's brother. How come?"

"They are hunting for you out there. His roadhouse is a stone's throw from the road. It is too dangerous," John Boy replied. "No. The only solution is to take our chances with the forest."

CHAPTER VI
THE WRANGLANDS

ⰶⱝⱑⰵⰵⱦⰵⰵⰵⰵ

The forest was too thick for Depper to trot. Instead, she took unusually dainty steps over the brush, snorting in annoyance. While the prince and princess rode, John Boy struggled to keep up on foot. Luke could barely believe that it had only been a day ago that they had been happy and comfortable. He would have laughed had someone told him then that he would soon be a refugee.

Luke swallowed hard when he thought about his father. Count Damien had said the king was dead. Luke tried to comprehend what that meant.

Luke remembered his father's face, his dark beard and his blue eyes that twinkled from beneath perpetually furrowed eyebrows. King Simon carried himself with a dignity that both impressed and intimidated Luke.

To the rest of the kingdom, the king was a leader, as strong as stone. To Luke he was all these things and more. For as long as he could remember, he always wanted to be like his father: Strong, courageous, good. That was the public king, the ruler, the wise judge.

There was another side to the king that his subjects never saw, but that Luke knew well. They loved to play hide and seek together and race up and down the long corridors. His father sometimes even played catch with him in the throne room, even though they had broken the beautiful stained glass windows more than once.

Luke tried to wrap his brain around the fact that his father was gone. Luke remembered one day in particular, when he had gotten his first glimpse of what it meant to be king.

Each year, fifty days after the anniversary of the High King's victory over death, any subject could bring his dispute before the king for justice. The king's judgment overrode that of the village council and other authorities.

That day, a widow came before the king, bringing her seven ragged children. The tax collector had seized her house, tossing her family out onto the streets. She explained that her husband had spent the tax money on drinking and gambling before he stumbled into the river and drowned.

"I will pay every penny I owe," she promised, throwing herself at the king's feet, "I just need a little more time."

The king had stroked his beard as his piercing eyes rested on her.

"I have already paid a quarter of what I owe," she begged. "Please, just give me more time."

Luke had been unimpressed by the woman. What kind of fool was she to marry such an irresponsible man? The woman's children had dirty faces, the prince noted with disapproval.

"How much do you still owe?" the king asked.

The woman told him. Fifty *lattens*.

Luke feigned a cough to cover his shocked laugh. His father shot him a stern glance. While nobles threw around that kind of money on everyday luxuries, it was more than an unskilled laborer could earn in a year.

How long has it been since this woman's husband paid his taxes? wondered Luke.

"I will pay your taxes this time," King Simon said. Then the king had reached into his pocket and pulled out a large gold coin. He leaned forward and handed it to her.

"Madam," he said, "on your way home, I want you to go to the cobbler and have him make a pair of shoes for each of your children. It will not do to have your children running barefoot during winter."

"Yes, sir, Your Highness, sir," the woman curtseyed clumsily as she backed away, disoriented by the king's mercy.

Luke had not even noticed that the woman's children were shoeless. The king later told him he had arranged for the woman to be employed as one of the palace weavers.

"Without a decent job," the king had explained, "that woman stands no chance at keeping those children fed on her own. Even if I only cared about money, it is still less costly to give her a good job than to have her work herself to death trying to pay her debt.

"How does it benefit me to have a half-dozen more orphans picking pockets in the streets? Besides, the High King said that He would only forgive our debts as much as we show mercy to others."

That was the day Luke had realized that being king was more than fun and games. Someday he would be king and would be responsible for all the people of Nèra Toli.

The idea of royal duty suddenly seemed terribly heavy. When he became king, he would rule his kingdom until the day he died, without breaks or vacations. Until the day he died . . .

It was then that it really hit Luke that his father was dead. He swallowed the tears that threatened to flood everywhere and clenched his fists in anger. Later on would be the time to mourn, but now he had to focus on surviving.

By law, he himself was the rightful new king. But what kind of king runs away from his enemy? Luke would have to face his destiny sooner or later: He was king, despite not even being old enough to shave.

Luke slowly awoke from his thoughts. He and his sister were still astride Depper, while John Boy huffed along beside the great horse. Despite the beautiful surroundings, Luke felt a creeping sense of claustrophobia. The canopy of trees blocked out the sky above.

He wished he knew what time of day it was. It felt noonish. Whatever the hour, it felt like it was time to eat. Luke's stomach growled loudly.

"Hungry?" asked John Boy. He shuffled through the knapsack, adding, "Well, we have sandwiches and apples. Which will it be?"

"Sandwich, please," Luke answered. "But we will have to get off this infernal beast for a while."

Depper neighed indignantly. John Boy calmed the great horse. "I'm afraid not," he said. "You see, this forest is far more dangerous than it looks."

"What do you mean? How is it dangerous at all?" Luke asked in annoyance.

"Did you grow up living in a cave somewhere?" John Boy murmured under his breath.

"In a castle, which is practically the same thing," Lexi retorted. "I would also like a sandwich, please."

"The forest is dangerous," John Boy said, "because of the faeries that live here. They steal any children that wander off alone. A while ago, Lexi thought that *she* chose to gather that bouquet of flowers. I'm sure you also thought *you* chose to climb that tree.

"Really, it was *them* making you want to do those things. They want to get you away from any grownups so they can grab you and steal you. This place is enchanted to make people forgetful and to make children wander off, away from their parents. It's the faeries."

"But why?" Luke asked. "What did we ever do to them? Why would they hurt us?"

"What did *you* ever do to them? Nothing," John Boy said, "but you are still heir to the fruit of your forefathers' deeds. When our ancestors came here a long time ago, they roused the faeries' wrath by felling thousands of trees to build their civilization. To us they are heroes who conquered this land and built our kingdom. To the faeries we are all villains. They steal children to plant a fear of the forest in our hearts."

"But if they only hurt children, what is to stop grownups from coming into the forest?" asked Lexi. "After all, it was the grown-ups that used to chop down the trees, right?"

"I didn't say the faeries hurt the children they steal," John Boy corrected. "Even still, they do more than steal children. If they see a woodsman or a hunter invade their forest, they make sure he won't enter the Wranglands a second time:

"They'll pelt him with acorns hard enough to bruise him all over. If he tries to fell a tree, the whole blade of his axe is liable to fly off mid-swing. Or, should he succeed in striking the tree, a rock somehow gets in the way and chips or shatters his blade."

"But a hunter could surely kill faeries, just as easily as killing a deer or a boar," Luke suggested.

"It's bad luck to harm faeries. Besides, they'll steal all a hunter's arrows before he can use them," John Boy whispered. "Faeries are right hard to see if they don't want to be seen. One could be right in front of your face and you wouldn't even know it.

"Even if you did see a faery, I daresay you wouldn't be able to move a muscle. You'd be frozen under its spell. No hunter with his head on straight would even enter these woods since the faeries hide all the game anyway."

"If faeries are so mean," said Lexi, "why have they left the three of us alone?"

"Yeah," Luke added, "I bet this is just a tale made up by a bunch of incompetent hunters and lazy woodcutters. If there were faeries all around us, they have made themselves known by now."

"Don't speak too soon," John Boy said, turning to Depper. She had become noticeably more irritable in the last few minutes. He rubbed her velvety nose to calm her. Depper tossed her head about and whinnied, stomping her feet defiantly.

SLAP! There came a loud sound from Depper's rear. The horse shot forward, knocking John Boy aside. Luke and Lexi held on for their lives.

Depper darted down embankments and up hills. The twins ducked to avoid being knocked off her back by low branches. The behemoth pounded onward for an eternity. When she finally started slowing down, it was out of exhaustion. Finally, she stopped walking and just stood in place.

After a long while, John Boy caught up with the great horse. He panted loudly.

"So, do you two have anything else you'd like to say about faeries?" John Boy demanded. "Or maybe you'd like to wait until Depper is rested and ready to run some more."

"I'm sorry," Luke apologized.

"Yeah, me too," added Lexi, examining her feet.

"We might as well give Depper a break and just stop here," John Boy said.

The prince and princess eagerly jumped down. John Boy warned them not to leave his sight, so they drank in the scenic forest from beside Depper. Lexi fished for a snack in the knapsack.

Lexi took a bite of an apple. She was so sick of apples. This was the first apple she had actually eaten, but the smell had made her sick since being stowed away the previous night.

She looked longingly at a particularly inviting blackberry bush in the distance. The berries looked so juicy. Lexi wondered if she would ever taste blackberry pie again. Then, at the base of the bush, Lexi noticed a bucket full of the plumpest, shiniest berries of all. She blinked, but the vision persisted.

"Follow me!" shouted Lexi, darting off into the woods. "This way! Come on!" She raced for the bucket of berries. It meant something. It meant that they were not alone in the faery-infested forest after all.

John Boy and Luke assumed that the princess had lost her senses, but followed anyway. Depper protested at having to leave the patch of succulent grass she had been chewing. John Boy yanked her along anyway.

He had no desire to lose his fine horse to the faeries. By the time they tramped over too where Lexi had been, she had disappeared again.

"Where has that girl got to now?" John Boy growled under his breath. Then he saw the clearing. The thick trees ended and the tall grass began. Lexi raced toward the meadow, trailed by her brother.

John Boy ran after them, yelling, "Stop! Listen to me, you two! Stop! That looks like a faery ring if ever I've seen one!"

Neither twin heard him. John Boy huffed his way toward the prince and princess. He was still trying to recover from chasing Depper and in no condition to begin another chase. Just then, his boot caught on an exposed root and the heavyset man landed hard on the ground. When he tried to stand up, his ankle throbbed intensely. By the time he could hobble to the blackberry bush, Luke and Lexi had already reached the meadow.

"I see a house!" Luke shouted back as he ran.

Chapter VII
THE DWARVES' DAUGHTER

Luke and Lexi stared. A log cabin seemed to grow out of the meadow before them. No, it was the other way around: Grass and wildflowers sprouted from the cabin's low roof.

The cabin itself looked very old. It seemed to be slowly sinking back into the sea of flowers. The twins' first thought was that it was abandoned. Then they noticed smoke rising from the chimney. The smell of dinner filled their nostrils.

"Do you suppose it's a faery house?" Lexi whispered, almost afraid the house would vanish if she spoke too loudly.

"Everyone knows that faeries live outdoors," Luke said knowingly. "Whoever lives there is as human as we are." He set out across the meadow, toward the little cabin.

"Where are you going?" Lexi cried.

"Where do you *think* I am going?" he called across the meadow. "I am going to see if anyone is home."

"But what if they are unfriendly?" Lexi shouted. "What if they know that about the bounty on our heads?

"Sis, if you want to talk to me, come here," Luke called. He was already on the other side of the meadow, near the little cabin. "I am hungry. I want something to eat besides apples."

"*Nar ainer!*" muttered the princess under her breath. She ran through the tall grass to catch up with her brother.

Just as Lexi crossed the meadow, John Boy limped to the edge of the trees. He leaned on Depper for support, wishing he could ride instead of walk. There was no way he could mount Depper with his ankle throbbing. The horse grazed contentedly on the sweet grass and flowers.

John Boy frantically scanned the clearing for the prince and princess. They were already at the cottage. What if a witch lived there? It was foolish to just go knocking on strangers' doors.

"Stop! Stay away from there!" he called.

Lexi called back, "If you want to talk to me, come here!"

"Don't you get smart with me, young lady!" John Boy shouted, hobbling across the meadow toward them. "You two may be royalty, but you're still children as far as I'm concerned!"

"It's no good," Luke said, plopping down on a roughly hewn bench beside the door. "No one is home. They probably deserted this place a long time ago."

"But I can see smoke coming from the chimney," Lexi observed. "Someone must be nearby. Let's just wait for them." She plopped down beside her brother to wait.

* * *

A moment later, the twins felt something smooth and cold at their necks. "Don't move and just maybe I won't kill you," came a female voice from behind them.

Out of the corner of his eye, Luke could see the blade at his sister's throat and could feel another below his own chin. He breathed short, nervous breaths.

"Who are you and what business do you have in these woods?" The girl demanded.

"We are travelers, nothing more," Lexi answered, trying to sound convincing.

"You are either very stupid or you are traveling wizards, that's all I can say," the girl laughed. "The only ones who venture south of the road are highwaymen waiting to ambush unsuspecting passersby. Even they stay within a score of feet from the road, if they have any brains.

"As for you being wizards: Ha! So, boy, tell me who you are, if you want to live to see the sun set today!"

"I am Prince Luke, son of His Majesty, King Simon. This is my sister, Princess Lexi," said Luke.

Luke and Lexi felt the pressure at their necks disappear. They turned around and saw their captor prostrate on the ground. Both blades lay in the dust in front of her.

"Forgive me, my Lord and Milady!" the girl cried. "I had no idea!"

"Come on. Get up," Luke said, taking the stranger's hand.

Her face was dusty and tear-stained, but her clear blue eyes sparkled at him. She had shoulder-length amber curls and wore plain clothes befitting any farmer's daughter. Luke gazed at her for a long time.

"What is your name?" he finally asked.

"I'm Megan, Megan Short," she replied, "and this is my home. Mother and Father will be so excited to meet you." She paused. "But what are you doing here in the Wranglands?"

"We should go inside," Luke answered. "We can talk more there."

Luke and Lexi had to stoop to enter the front door. So did Megan, but she ducked so gracefully as to be almost imperceptible.

Remembering the grass growing from the cabin's roof, Lexi looked up, expecting to see a ceiling of soil. Instead, she saw log beams above her. Looking around, she saw that the whole cabin consisted of one large room with an earthen floor.

A crackling fire burned in the large stone fireplace that dominated the left-hand wall. A simmering cauldron hung over the fire, smelling of a hearty stew.

There was little in the way of furniture, and what furniture there was seemed oddly diminutive. To her right she saw two beds. One was long and narrow; the other was short and wide, complete with two pillows.

"Your Highnesses, I'd like you to meet my parents, Goodman and Goodwife Short," said Megan. She motioned toward two chairs that faced the fire. A round head appeared over each chair's armrest.

"Mama, Papa," she said, "please meet the prince and princess."

A small, plump woman hopped down from her chair and waddled over to the royal siblings. Meanwhile, a little bearded man put down his pipe and got to his feet, mindful of his large middle. The miniature woman curtseyed awkwardly before the twins.

"So pleased to meet you, Prince Luke and Princess Lexi!" the little woman said excitedly.

Luke reached out both hands toward her. To the woman's surprise, the prince shook her hand vigorously.

"Glad to meet you, Goodwife Short!" he grinned.

Lexi tried to shake the woman's hand while gaping at her, dumbfounded. Lexi herself was barely five feet tall, but Megan's mother was a good foot-and-a-half shorter still.

"Pleased!" Lexi said awkwardly. She had never been this close to a dwarf before and was sure she was being horribly rude by staring. At the same time, she simply could not tear her eyes away from her hosts.

"I'm honored by your presence, Your Highnesses!" Megan's father added. Before the dwarf could bow, Luke seized his small hand, gripping it warmly.

"How wonderful to meet you, Goodman Short!" the prince said. "You have a quite a courageous daughter."

Lexi still remembered Megan's cold blade at her neck. The princess cleared her throat. Courageous was not quite the word she would have chosen.

"And you must be Princess Lexi," the little man said.

He was only slightly taller than his wife, so he still had to crane his neck to look up at her. Since it seemed shaking hands was now the fashion, Lexi reluctantly clasped his stubby fingers in her own.

"Yes, and I take it that you are Goodman *Short,*" Lexi involuntarily choked on the last word.

"Aye, miss, 'tis true what you're thinking," he answered. "I'm a dwarf, and so is my dear wife here. Have a good look, then. All right, are you satisfied?"

Goodwife Short glanced sternly at her husband. *He should be more polite, even if their guests were not,* she thought. *He should be used to the stares by now.*

"Well, then," said Megan, "you must be exhausted. I'm afraid we only have three chairs, but the bed is also comfortable to sit on."

Just then came a furious pounding at the front door. The whole cottage shook.

"Let them go!" thundered a voice from outside. "Touch one hair on their heads and your lives will be forfeit!"

"It's John Boy!" cried Lexi. "Quick! Let him in!"

Megan unbolted the door before John Boy could pound it down. John Boy burst into the room, panting and limping like a wounded grizzly bear.

CHAPTER VIII
WESTWARD BY MOONLIGHT

ꝗꝗꝗ ꝗꝗꝗ ꝗꝗꝗ ꝗꝗꝗ ꝗꝗꝗ

For a moment, everyone stared in silence at John Boy. His heavy breathing pulsated through the room. At last, John Boy calmed down enough to speak.

"How much have you told them?" he demanded, trying to read Luke and Lexi's faces. John Boy looked red all over, with beads of sweat dripping down his forehead.

"Nothing yet," Lexi said, "but we have to tell them something."

"We did happen to mention our identities," Luke added. Lexi scowled at him.

"Tell them nothing more!" John Boy spat. He took another step toward the twins, but buckled when he put weight on his right leg. He crumbled to the ground in pain.

Megan fearlessly rushed forward. She helped John Boy over to the low bed, where he sank into the straw mattress. Goodwife Short made a poultice for John Boy's swollen ankle while Megan pulled off his boots.

"Now what's all this secrecy about?" Megan asked sweetly. "Why aren't the prince and princess traveling in style, but instead sneaking through the forest like a couple of thieves?"

"Trust no one!" John Boy harrumphed and turned away.

Megan looked to Luke. "Someone please give us some answers," she implored. "You are guests in our home. The least you could do is explain why you're here, where you're going and what this is all about."

Luke took a deep breath and began.

"Everyone is looking for us," he said. "I expect they will be pounding down your door any minute. You can't let them find us."

"I don't understand," Megan replied. "Why not?"

"They want to arrest us!" Lexi interrupted.

"Lexi!" John Boy shouted.

"Oh shut up, you big oaf!" said Goodwife Short, tending to his ankle. "Let them tell their story."

Luke continued, "Last night our father was murdered. I would bet the kingdom that it was Count Damien, our father's no-good advisor. But he made it seem like *we* are the guilty ones! So we have run away and have nowhere to go."

"But what now?" asked Megan. "Surely, you must have some plan, some idea of what you're going to do next."

"There was a plan," Luke said, "but it has gone all wrong. We were supposed to meet our Nana's brother, but he lives along the road, where Damien's henchmen are searching for us.

"I think the bigger plan was to get to our tutor Timothy and beg for help. Just yesterday we found out that he was sent away by Count Damien."

"Do you know where to find this Timothy of yours?" Megan pressed. "Maybe we can help you get to him."

Just then Megan's father spoke. "I don't think it would be wise for you children to go anywhere," he said authoritatively.

"This is just about the safest place in the entire forest, and the forest is a great deal safer than the road. You'll just be staying here, that's what." The old dwarf puffed his pipe as if that settled the matter.

"Count Damien murdered our father!" Lexi interrupted. "We refuse to just hide. He will take over the whole kingdom unless we stop him, and the only way we can do that is with the help of a powerful magician!"

"You'll get yourselves killed if you leave this house," Goodman Short answered. "I forbid you to leave."

"We escape Count Damien only to be held prisoners by a couple of dwarves!" cried Lexi in exasperation.

"All right, you two," said Goodwife Short, "let's stop this arguing and see about a little something for dinner. Tonight we're having stew and potatoes, and you'll not bicker anymore in my house."

* * *

Later on, when everyone was getting ready for bed, Megan approached Luke.

"Do you have any idea where your tutor, this magician, has gone off to?" she asked.

"We think he has gone into exile, probably among the hermits who dwell in the Saw Tooth Mountains," said Luke, "but he has been gone for only two days. Maybe we can still catch him on his way there."

"And this brother of your nurse's," Megan probed, "where along the road does he live?"

"I have no idea, but John Boy knows," answered Luke. "We could ask him."

"No, no, no," whispered Megan. "He'll either want to go as well, or want us to stay here. Either way, he's bound to blow our cover."

"I think I remember Nana mentioning one time that her brother's roadhouse served the best hash browns in all of Nėra Toli. Does that mean anything to you?" Luke said hopefully.

"Yes, I know the place!" Megan cried, before continuing in a hushed tone. "That's the Beaten Path Roadhouse! It's right on the road, about ten miles from here. It'll be dangerous, but Nana's brother might know where to find Timothy. I think we should chance it."

"Enough chatter, my kidlets!" Goodwife Short interrupted. "Megan, I need your help making beds for our guests."

Megan reluctantly joined her mother in stuffing large burlap sacks with straw. Lexi watched with fascination as they worked. She had never seen anyone stuff a mattress before, much less with anything as undignified as straw.

Soon her brother pulled her aside and told her the escape plan. Lexi glanced over at John Boy, who had relaxed and sat chatting with Goodman Short. Lexi felt reassured to see that John Boy seemed oblivious to their scheming.

Before long, it was time for bed. Goodwife Short pulled the royal twins aside.

"I wish I could offer both of you real beds to sleep in," she said. "Since Megan's bed is the only one big enough to accommodate someone with long legs, I'd like to offer that one to our future king."

I'm the firstborn, Lexi thought bitterly. *I should be first in line for the throne. I should be first in line to be offered a bed to sleep in.*

Despite her anger, she tried not to hate her brother. It wasn't his fault he was a boy. It wasn't his fault that the whole system was unfair in Nėra Toli. But still, he didn't seem to be arguing.

"Lexi, John Boy and Megan, here are your beds," Goodwife Short motioned to three straw-filled sacks, each covered with a worn blanket.

While everyone else seemed to fall asleep almost as soon as they got in bed, Luke struggled in vain to get comfortable. Straw poked through the bedclothes into his back like needles. He was wondering if he would ever drift off when he heard his sister whispering to herself.

"Horrible bed!" she grumbled. "How do these peasants ever sleep?"

"Hey, Sis!" Luke whispered. "I can't sleep either."

"At least you are in a bed, Mister Future King!" Lexi said bitterly, rolling over to face away from him.

"You know that is not my fault," Luke sighed. "Besides, I doubt this straw is any more comfortable with or without a bed frame under it. We should both just try and get some sleep, okay?"

"Okay," Lexi quietly replied. "Sorry for being nasty."

"I forgive you, Sis," Luke yawned. "Goodnight."

Just when he had finally nodded off, Luke found himself being shaken awake. "Wake up," breathed Megan. "It's time for us to go."

A few minutes later, Luke, Lexi and Megan were out the door. Goodman and Goodwife Short still slept soundly, while John Boy snored loudly. The three shadowy figures tiptoed to the stables.

The twins got Depper ready. Megan had slipped off somewhere, so Lexi went to fetch her. Lexi found Megan crouched down, milking one of several miniature goats. The princess had never seen such a small dairy goat before.

"Megan! What are you doing?" Lexi asked, incredulous. "We have no time for you to do your morning chores!"

"Relax! If I don't milk them, they'll be raising a ruckus by sunup. Then my parents will be up and hot on our trail," Megan calmly replied, milking as she spoke.

Luke led Depper out of the stable. It was still dark outside, without the slightest hint of light in the east. He turned to his sister and Megan.

"For now, only two of us should ride Depper at a time," he said. "We don't want to wear her out when our own legs have a few miles in them."

"I think you're right," said Megan, "especially since she's also carrying our gear."

"But it is ten miles to the roadhouse!" cried Lexi. "That is much too far to walk!"

"I will take the first turn walking," said Luke.

"Come on, you two," Megan pressed. "We have to go now if we don't want Mom and Dad to wake up and notice we're missing." She led Depper to the front porch.

Megan climbed up onto Depper from the bench. Lexi followed, but her eyes lingered on the bench for an extra moment. The day before, she had felt Megan's cold blade pressed against her throat.

Now Megan seemed infinitely nicer than in those first few moments, but Lexi still wondered how much they could trust her. Lexi climbed up behind Megan.

"All right," Luke cleared his throat, as if taking charge. "Which way are we going?"

"Let's head west through the forest and then, when we've gone ten miles, we'll head north to the road," Megan suggested.

"But how will we know when we have gone ten miles?" asked Lexi. "There are no signs or landmarks, just trees."

"This is my home," Megan replied. "I know every tree and rock. I'll know when we've gone far enough."

"Do you think your parents would mind if I borrowed this?" Luke asked, showing Megan a walking stick that stood as tall as he did.

"I'm sure they wouldn't mind," Megan said, "if it were theirs. But since it's mine, you can definitely use it."

"Oh, thanks," he replied.

"It would be a little tall for my parents, don't you think?" Megan added, smiling. "Come on then, let's go before we wake the rooster. He'll blow our cover." She quickly pressed her heels to the horse's sides and Depper moved forward.

Dawn was still far off when they set out. Stars twinkled through the canopy of trees above them. The hours passed slowly as they hurried along in the darkness. Luke and Lexi had never been outside of the castle at night before. Both silently wished that they could go home.

The looming darkness filled Lexi with a nameless fear. Her brother held a lamp in his left hand and the walking stick in his right. The flame flickered comfortingly, but its light seemed insignificant against the pressing blackness of the trees.

Lexi still felt a nagging fear that there was something out there watching them, hunting them. Whatever it was out there, it scared her even more than the idea of being taken by Count Damien's men. Lexi shivered. They traveled in silence, with only their lamp to stave off the darkness.

"Let's have a bite to eat before we go any further," Megan suggested after a while. Luke and Lexi both jumped when she broke the silence.

"There is something out there," Luke said. "It avoids the light, but I know it is there."

"So it's not just me," Lexi said, relieved that someone else felt the same way she did.

"No," answered Luke. "I feel it too."

Just then, *it* passed between the trees again. The eyes of a giant black wolf flashed in the light and, in another instant, the wolf had melted back into the shadows.

CHAPTER IX
AN UNEXPECTED ALLY

𝔚𝔢𝔩𝔵𝔢𝔭𝔠𝔯𝔮𝔢𝔩𝔯𝔶 𝔷𝔬𝔰𝔯𝔶 𝔷𝔞𝔯𝔯𝔞𝔯𝔞𝔷𝔠

Lexi screamed and the great horse reared, neighing loudly. Luke turned white beneath his freckles. He clutched his walking stick more firmly than ever.

"What *was* that?" Luke demanded shakily.

Megan alone seemed to keep her cool. She answered in a low voice, "That was Wolfram, the guardian of the forest. He's just curious about what we're doing here. He won't hurt us."

"That monster is hunting us, I tell you!" Luke snapped. "Make it go away!"

"Wolfram won't go away. He will watch us as long as we're in the forest, to make sure that we don't harm any of his friends," Megan answered.

Lexi calmed Depper, patting the great beast's neck. The horse still pranced nervously.

"What friends?" Lexi asked. "You and your family are the only people we've seen since we entered this forest."

"Of course you can't expect to see them unless they want you to—same as with Wolfram," said Megan. "They're shy of people and especially suspicious of strangers."

"Who?" Luke demanded angrily. "Who are they? Who is this wolf that stalks us?"

"*They* are the Fair Folk, or faeries. Wolfram is a large black wolf the faeries raised from a pup," Megan said. "Wolfram seems wary of us, though he's seen me often enough. He might relax a little if I explain our quest."

"Let's get going again," pleaded Lexi. "No good ever came of trying to reason with savage beasts."

A low growl emanated from the bushes.

"Be careful what you say," said Megan. "You might hurt his feelings. Wolfram can be very emotional."

"Are you telling me that this creature understands everything we say?" Luke asked incredulously.

"Wolves are very intelligent, and Wolfram is as smart as they come," Megan answered. "Now let me try and calm him down. Then one of you can explain things." She began to sing in a lilting voice:

"To pass unhindered through your land
Is all we ask today.
Had we a bit more time at hand,
We promise we would stay
To dance and feast as you demand
Until we're old and gray.
In haste we make this trip unplanned
And for your blessing pray."

After Megan finished, Luke realized that it was his turn to address the unseen wolf.

"Please stop frightening us like that, watching us from the shadows," he said. "We mean no harm to you or your faery friends.

"We are trying to avenge our father's murder and stop his killer from taking over the kingdom," Luke continued. "We are only traveling through the forest to avoid our enemies. They are afraid to set foot here, and now I see why."

"I am sure you are much nicer than you seem," added Lexi hopefully. "I hope you will forgive me if I have hurt your feelings. I meant no harm."

Just beyond the reach of the lamplight, they all glimpsed a moving shadow. Then the giant wolf entered the ring of light.

Lexi gasped. It walked right up beside Depper and sat down tamely. The giant horse was too frightened to do anything.

Luke stared at the huge wolf before him. Although the wolf was sitting down, its head was higher than Luke's own. He had never seen such a large dog or wolf. It was bigger than some ponies.

Megan and Lexi still sat astride Depper. Megan looked down calmly at the giant canine. When Lexi finally got up the courage to look down, she found that the great beast was looking straight at her. She gasped.

Her first instinct was to look away, but she forced herself to meet his gaze. Only then did she see that Wolfram, this huge wolf, had the sweet eyes of a puppy. He opened his mouth, exposing his long fangs, and spoke.

"Hello, girl," he said. "Your brother is tired and would like to ride the horse. Come down and I will carry you to wherever you are going."

"But what if I come down and you eat me?" said Lexi. "I have heard lots of stories about wolves."

"Am I devouring your brother?" replied the wolf. "I am sure one child tastes just as good as another, but then I do not eat children so I would not know."

Lexi looked at her brother to gather her courage. If anything went wrong, surely Luke would protect her—or die trying.

"Relax, Sis," Luke said at last. "Everything is going to be all right. I have a feeling that Wolfram is on our side."

"Okay," Lexi whispered to herself and slid down off Depper's back. As she stood looking at Wolfram, she realized how immense he was. He was bigger than any wolf she had ever seen.

She reached out to him, letting him first sniff her hand, and then ran her fingers through his long black fur. Lexi scratched behind his ears a little, which made him really seem like a puppy.

"So how in Nèra Toli am I going to get up onto your back?" she asked.

In answer, Wolfram lay down, which really made him seem doggish. Lexi thought of her father's lapdog. That dog could sit just fine, but would never lie down on command. Even though the little dog was so difficult to train, her father adored it.

Much to Queen Tabitha's chagrin, the king even let that lapdog sleep on the royal bed. It would prance around in the morning, waiting for its master to wake up. It pained Lexi to think of that annoying little dog prancing around her father's dead body, not understanding why he wouldn't wake up.

He will never wake up again! she thought bitterly. Lexi climbed on the great wolf's back. In a moment, Wolfram rose and stood on all fours.

A few minutes later, Luke and Megan sat astride Depper. Lexi examined them critically. Every movement, every expression betrayed their fondness for one another. Luke smoothed one of Megan's loose locks of hair back into place.

Lexi turned away, embarrassed. It was scandalous how little regard her brother had for his betrothal. At the same time, the princess wished she had some alternative to the arranged marriage that awaited her.

"We're heading to the Beaten Path Roadhouse, but we want to go through the forest as far as possible," Megan explained to Wolfram.

"You are on the right track then," the wolf answered, "but we had better hurry if we plan on getting there before broad daylight."

At that, the wolf began running down the path. Lexi gripped his fur for dear life. Depper, who now carried Luke and Megan, neighed and galloped after him.

Within an hour, they were almost at the roadhouse. The miles of forest had wisped by in the fleeting shadows, like a vague dream.

Wolfram and Lexi were the first to emerge through the foliage and up onto the road. Wolfram sniffed. Lexi peered to the left and to the right.

The sun and royal palace both hid beyond the horizon, but the eastern sky was beginning to glow. Turning to her left, Lexi still saw a few stars glowing in the western sky. In either direction, no living creature stirred.

"The coast is clear," Wolfram called back to the bushes.

In a moment, Depper emerged from the trees, carrying Luke and Megan. All three seemed bluish in the predawn light, as Lexi watched them. Then she followed their gaze across the wide dirt road. There stood the roadhouse.

Wolfram and Lexi crossed the road first, followed by their companions. Luke dismounted the great golden brown horse and helped Megan down.

Wolfram lay down again and Lexi climbed off his big, shaggy back. Megan and the twins all looked at the roadhouse. The only structure for miles, it looked ominous in the predawn shadows. They all walked toward the front door.

Luke went to knock at the front door, but it was already slightly open. He slowly pushed it the rest of the way open.

"Hello! Is there anyone here?" he called, looking around. Everything lay topsy-turvy. Some stools and tables were broken and smashed.

"Count Damien's men have already been here," Luke said, voicing his companions' thoughts.

"But what does this mean?" asked Megan. "Wasn't your contact supposed to instruct you what to do next?"

"Our contact is probably on his way to the gallows," Lexi lamented.

"Calm down, Sis," Luke reassured her. "I am pretty sure that old Timothy has gone off to the Saw Tooth Mountains. All we have to do is follow the road up the mountain pass to where the hermit caves are. How complicated can it be?"

Just then, a door creaked. Lexi looked around but saw nothing. Then she heard footsteps. She turned to her brother. She could tell from his expression that he had heard the noise too.

Megan picked up a broom that had been leaning against the wall. Luke grabbed a poker from next to the fireplace. No one breathed as they walked toward the source of the sound. In the next room, the floorboards groaned under some heavy weight.

They kicked open the door in front of them and proceeded slowly through the doorway. Armed with his poker, Luke entered the kitchen first. The floor creaked again. Megan and Lexi followed.

An instant later, they saw him: a great, terrible shape to their right. The next instant passed in slow motion. An immense, scraggly man lunged at Luke, wildly swinging a heavy sword. Lexi and Megan screamed in terror.

Chapter X
THE PATH THROUGH THE MOUNTAINS

𝒵𝒶𝟥𝓊𝒶Ωℓ𝒸𝒶ⁱℓ𝒾𝓃𝓇θ𝒪𝓍𝒹ⁱℓℓ

The burly man was almost on top of Luke when a dark shape knocked the prince aside. By the time the prince was back on his feet, the attacker lay on the floor with a huge, snarling wolf on his chest. The attacker's sword was lodged in the wall, where it had been hurled in the scuffle.

"Wolfram, don't kill him!" called Megan urgently. "Not yet!"

"Why not?" snarled Wolfram. His eyes held an unfamiliar, half-crazed ferocity.

Lexi suddenly realized that, when she first saw Wolfram, she had sensed that this rage lurked somewhere inside him. It scared her. Worse yet, she realized that she recognized his anger. Somewhere deep down, she too had this same rage.

"We need to ask him some questions," Megan insisted. "He's no use to us dead."

Lexi looked at the man. Wolfram still stood on the stranger's thick chest, snarling into his face. The man had dark, uncombed hair and several days' worth of stubble on his chin. His face was twisted in fear and tears poured down from his black eyes.

Even though this man was their enemy and had been sent to kill them, Lexi still felt a little sorry for him. In ambushing them, he had just been obeying orders. He probably believed that Luke and Lexi really were assassins deserving death.

"What is your name?" Lexi asked, kneeling down and drying the man's tears.

"Zared," he whimpered pathetically.

Megan pulled the sword from the wall and pointed it at Zared's neck.

"All right, Zared," said Megan sternly. "Who sent you? What happened to everyone here? Talk!"

* * *

"Count Damien knew the king's murderers were coming here and meeting someone. He didn't know who their contact person was, so he had everyone here arrested.

"I was told to wait for you," said Zared, the blade inches was from his jugular. "He didn't think you would still come, but left me just in case. He said he wanted the prince and princess dead or alive, but that dead was simpler."

"How did Count Damien know the prince and princess were coming here at all?" Megan demanded, prodding Zared's neck with the sword.

"Their nurse," the guard answered.

"Nana betrayed us!" Luke cried out in shock. "How could she help us get away one minute and then go turn us in the next?"

"The nurse wasn't exactly cooperative," Zared added. "She took a lot of . . . convincing. Count Damien did promise her that no harm would come to you kids. She's even more simple-minded than she looks."

Most of Lexi's newfound compassion for the stranger evaporated, replaced by anger. She wanted to kick him in the ribs, but turned away instead. Megan still held the sword to the guard's throat and Wolfram remained standing on his chest, growling.

"Wolfram," said Luke, "can you watch this guy for a minute? The three of us need to talk."

Once they were in the next room, Lexi blurted out, "What do we do now? Where are we supposed to go next?"

"We know that Timothy will be an ally," said Luke. "Nana said he would be in the Saw Tooth Mountains, holed up in one of the hermit caves."

"Megan, how far west of the castle are we right now?" Lexi asked.

"A day's ride, I'd say," replied Megan.

"That far?" Luke said, surprised.

"That means that we still have a hundred miles to the base of the mountains," said Megan, "After that, the road to the High Pass is easily another hundred miles of steep, rocky trails."

"How in Nèra Toli are we going to get all the way there and back in time to prevent Count Damien from marrying Mom and making himself king!" Lexi cried.

"The wedding is on Sunday, right?" asked Megan.

"Right," said Lexi.

"Which leaves us with five days, counting today," said Luke.

"We simply can't do it!" Lexi interrupted.

"But it looks like our only choice..." Luke said.

"Can I make a suggestion?" Megan asked. "Why take the high road at all? There is another, much shorter road through the mountains."

"What are you talking about?" Lexi said doubtfully. "I have never heard of any other road."

"Neither have I," added Luke.

"If I tell you more, you mustn't ever tell anyone else. Knowledge of this road is a closely guarded secret," whispered Megan. "The king knew of it, but I doubt anyone else in his court did."

"Okay, okay," Lexi nodded. "We promise to keep it quiet—now tell us about this road. Besides, Dad himself would have told us about it sooner or later."

"From the base of the Saw Tooth Mountains, there is a hidden road through the mountains," Megan said. "This road goes all the way to Unicorn Valley, all the way to the caves where the hermits dwell. It is an ancient road—older than your father's kingdom—and known only to a few people."

"If it is older than the kingdom of Nèra Toli, was it built by the First Ones who live in Unicorn Valley?" asked Luke.

"No," answered Megan. "This road was built by people before them, but no one knows who those people were. The First Ones have stories about mighty beings who lived in this land in the beginning of time, before our ancestors came from across the sea. The First Ones say those beings built the road."

"Right . . ." Luke said skeptically.

"What is so fabulous about these roads that makes everyone even care who built them and when?" Lexi asked impatiently.

"The secret road is special," Megan explained, "because it goes under the mountains, through solid rock. Going through the Caverns of Atsash will save us at least two days of walking."

"Unbelievable!" Luke protested. "The Saw Tooth Mountains are almost solid granite. Even the limestone parts would take forever to cut through."

"I think Megan is just pulling our leg," said Lexi. "We have no time for old travelers' tales. I thought you were helping us, Megan, not making fun."

Megan looked hard at the twins. She seemed pretty serious for someone who was joking.

"I can't think of any way to prove this road exists, other than showing it to you," Megan said. "This is the safest—and shortest—way to Unicorn Valley.

"Count Damien's men are surely patrolling the mountain roads. They're looking for you, and if you stay above ground, they'll find you. If you actually want to get to this old Timothy of yours, you'll come with me."

"She has a point," Lexi said to her brother.

"Besides, unless we speed things up, we have no chance of getting help before the wedding," Luke said. "All right, the Caverns of Atsash it is!

* * *

At that, all three returned to the kitchen; they still had to deal with the man sent to murder them. Wolfram no longer stood on the man's chest. Instead, Zared sat huddled in a corner. The giant canine lay nearby, snarling occasionally.

"We're leaving soon and need to do something about this Zared fellow," Megan said to Wolfram, motioning toward the captive.

"Right," replied the wolf. "I'll rip out his throat, nice and easy." Wolfram rose and approached the trembling guard.

"No! I will not have him killed!" Lexi protested. "He is no threat to us now. To kill him now would be murder."

"This man will go straight to Count Damien and tell him that we're here!" argued Megan. "He'll be the death of us!"

Wolfram growled at the man, saying nothing more to Lexi. It was obvious that he disliked the idea of letting the guard live. Lexi looked to her brother for help. The expression on his face showed that he also thought they should do away with the guard.

"Sure, this man tried to kill us, but he failed," Lexi argued. "Now we hold his life in our hands. You want to murder him because he is in our way. He can tell Count Damien that we were here, but what more can he do?

"If we kill him, his dead body will betray our presence just as well." Lexi paused and went on. "This man probably has a wife and children. What did they do wrong to deserve to lose him? I thought we were the good guys . . ."

The man looked up from the corner. He saw his fate being decided before his eyes.

"Please don't kill me!" he begged. "I'm sorry for trying to hurt you all. I am a father. I have two beautiful little girls. Please!" The man collapsed in a heap of blubbering sobs.

Luke looked away. Now the man had both a name and a family. His common sense said that Zared was too dangerous to let live, but he knew that Lexi would never give in.

"All right, Sis. You want to spare him; *you* tie him up. We're leaving in five minutes," Luke finally said.

Lexi scrambled around for some rope and bound the guard securely. Everyone else went outside, but Lexi lingered for one last guilty look at the prisoner.

"I'd like to thank you for saving my life," Zared ventured. "Could I trouble you for just one more favor? Could you leave me some water? It could be days before anyone finds me. I could die of thirst before anyone comes. Please . . ."

A pitcher of water and an empty glass stood on the table. The princess filled the glass and set it on the floor beside to the bound guard.

"It is not much, but I hope it keeps you alive," Lexi said.

"Thank you so much, Your Highness!" the guard fawned. "You've been of more help than you can ever realize."

The princess left the kitchen and went outside to meet her companions. It felt good that she had been able to save the guard's life and ensure that he wouldn't die of thirst. She smiled to herself. Still, something about Zared bothered her.

* * *

When the princess stepped outside, she saw Luke and Megan hastily back away from each other. Lexi was sure they had been kissing. So her suspicions had been correct: Luke and Megan were falling for each other.

"Glad you could join us," said Megan. "Saying goodbye to the captive? I'm sure he'll always appreciate how we spared his life, but that won't stop him from killing us if he ever gets another chance."

"He would not!" Lexi protested, but she suspected that Megan was right. Then, just for spite, she added, "By the way, I hope you know that my brother is betrothed."

"You would be better off worrying about your own marriage, Sis," Luke said, glaring at her.

Lexi blushed. No one said anything else after that.

* * *

They looked west toward the mountains. By the time they left the roadhouse, it was already midmorning. Megan and Luke rode Depper, while Wolfram carried Lexi.

They crossed the road and returned to the cover of the forest. There, they followed trails that were all but invisible, but that Wolfram seemed to know well.

Despite the beauty of the forest, Lexi thought of Zared, tied up on the floor of the roadhouse kitchen. She hoped they had done the right thing in sparing his life. She thought about how she had left him that glass of water and wondered if she had made a mistake.

What good would it have done to have spared his life, only to have him die of dehydration? she thought.

Still, the more she thought it over, the more she felt she had made a mistake. She felt as if she should tell the others what she had done, but she held back.

After her last exchange with her brother and Megan, she had no desire to give them any more ammunition to use against her.

CHAPTER XI
THE FAERY QUEEN'S BANQUET

꒰꒱

Rare and beautiful flowers filled the forest, but Lexi hardly noticed them. Her vague, uncomfortable feeling about Zared had turned into a vague, uncomfortable feeling about everything.

She still disliked the idea of taking the road under the mountains. Sure, Megan seemed nice enough, but what if it was a trap? They had known Megan for less than a day. How could they trust her with their lives?

Lexi was worried about her brother. He was obviously infatuated with that dwarf-born peasant.

There was no way he could see clearly now. Megan could lead him anywhere and he would follow.

The princess thought of her brother's seven-year-old bride-to-be. Even though it would be at least another half-dozen years before the wedding, the contract had been finalized.

What in Nèra Toli was Luke thinking? Courting a peasant when he was already promised to a princess! As much as Lexi detested the idea of being given in marriage without her consent, that was the way the world worked.

The princess looked up as wispy clouds raced westward ahead of her. She thought again of the road ahead. No matter what Megan said, the idea of being in a strange, close space felt unsafe.

The last thing Lexi wanted to do was to travel scores of miles without the sky above her. All of her instincts said it was better to stay out in the open, warmed by the late spring sun.

By early afternoon, Lexi's stomach grumbled loudly. Wolfram, who still carried the princess on his shaggy back, spoke up. "Your stomach sounds like it is part-wolf," he said. "That is some ferocious growling."

"I refuse to be the one to make us stop and eat," Lexi answered. "We are in a bit of a hurry, you know."

"Luke! Megan!" Wolfram called ahead. "When are we be stopping for lunch?"

"I was just thinking about that," Luke answered. "It looks like there is a nice little clearing up ahead. That will be a good place to rest."

A few minutes later, the travelers were all lounging in the large, round clearing. Toward the middle of the lawn, the grass was short and yellowish, but around the edge, it grew tall and thick. The long grass was still moist with the morning dew, so they spread a blanket.

Wolfram lost no time in scouring the woods for a snack. Depper grazed on a juicy patch of grass, while Megan unwrapped one of her bundles.

"Here we have some sandwiches," said Megan, distributing food. Soon everyone was eating.

Lexi felt so nice and relaxed that she lay back, with her head on the thick tufts of grass. She could see wild mushrooms growing just beyond the ring of grass and she wondered whether they were edible.

With great effort, she looked over at her brother and Megan. They were already taking a nap. Lexi wondered why she was yawning when she was not really tired—only a little bit dizzy—but she was asleep before she knew it.

* * *

Luke opened his eyes. Everything around him seemed hazy and surreal. He found himself seated at a long table. It was hard to tell how long it was, but it went on and on to the left and right until disappearing in the mist.

White candles in golden candlesticks decorated the table in both directions, looking shorter in the distance. The white tablecloth was strewn with decorative sheaves of dried, golden wheat.

The table was clearly being set for some banquet, since servants kept coming to and fro, always bringing more covered, steaming plates of food. Luke soon spotted Megan and Lexi further down the table on either side.

Lexi still slept heavily, with her head on the table. Megan, in contrast, looked terrified. Rising to go to her, Luke discovered that his legs would not move. The prince looked down: Leather straps bound each leg to his luxurious chair!

When Luke glanced up again, he saw a beautiful, frightening face across the table. Then he saw the *others*. All the seats near him were filled with staring faces.

Every last seat along the length of the table had been filled instantly. Luke wondered what manner of sorcery was at work. Suddenly, up and down the table, every candle ignited.

The prince felt disoriented and confused. *This must be a dream,* he thought. *How do I wake up?*

The woman still stared at him. He met her eyes and felt them burn him. Luke wanted to look away, but forced himself to hold her gaze.

His eyes watered, but still he did not back down. The woman's eyes were a very pale blue and her skin was as white as paper. Her hair, in contrast, was a lustrous black. As Luke observed the strange woman, her penetrating eyes lost their strength to intimidate him.

"Welcome to my realm," the woman finally said. "Are you enjoying yourself?"

"Maybe I would be, if you treated us with more hospitality," Luke retorted.

"How am I not being hospitable?" the woman said mockingly. "Look at the feast I am holding in your honor. I even grace you with my presence, yet you are ungrateful."

"You have kidnapped my friends and me. A good hostess does not have to tie up her dinner guests," said Luke. He motioned toward Megan and Lexi, certain that they were also bound.

Luke glanced down at his lap again. His legs were no longer bound with leather straps, but with iron—no, golden—shackles. Some strange magic was definitely at work.

"Are you aware, dear Prince, that you are trespassing?" asked the woman.

"What are you talking about?" Luke furrowed his brows. "This is *my* kingdom."

The woman assumed a grave expression. "These lands belong to the trees and the faeries," she continued. "You have no business being here. You are fortunate that I have not already killed you for being a spy."

"You know that I am the prince, yet you claim that I am trespassing when I have not even left my own kingdom," said Luke. "Besides, if I am unwelcome because I am human, how do you explain why *you* are here? You are neither faery nor tree."

"Obviously, no one has bothered teaching you history. It is a useful subject to master, unless you enjoy being a fool," the woman said. She took a bite of food and chewed for an eternity before continuing.

"I am Alysia, mother of this forest, guardian of the faeries. I was once a woman, but now I rarely appear as one. When I do not look like this, I am a fir tree."

"How can you be mother to an entire forest?" Luke asked doubtfully.

"The trees here are my children and the children of my children. But I do not want to talk about my history, but yours," she said. Alysia took another bite. "I suggest that you eat something, it is a long story."

Luke looked down at his plate. It was filled with the most succulent delicacies he had ever seen, but he resisted even tasting them.

He knew that faery food was often enchanted and could cause one to sleep for a century, waking only to find one's family and friends long dead of old age. Although his stomach rumbled, Luke ate nothing.

"Very well. Perhaps you will change your mind in a week or two," said Alysia. "Now you claim this forest as part of your kingdom. I believe you call it the Wranglands. Do you know why, dear Prince, your people do not use timber from this forest?"

"Because the trees are misgrown and good for nothing," Luke spat. "Everyone knows that! That is why they are called the Wranglands."

"You have been misled, my boy," the faery queen continued. "Why do your people fear to even enter these woods, do you know that?"

Now Luke was less sure. "I have heard that they are haunted," he said. "People say that the faeries will steal children who wander inside the forest's bounds. Even grown men are afraid of this place. No one talks about it."

"Ah!" Alysia smiled. "I see there is a grain of truth mixed in with the lies they teach you. Would you like to hear about what really happens to children who come into this forest?"

"Not really," Luke yawned defiantly.

The queen ignored him. "Many years ago," she began, "when this land was young and unburdened by the history of men, this forest stretched from the Southern Sea all the way to the Icy Mountains. There were already people living in this land, but they took only what they needed and cared for the forest.

"Then your people came south across the mountains, leaving the Cold Place behind. You saw this land as a thing to be conquered and tamed. You began slaughtering trees to build your dead houses.

"At first, we trees were at a loss for what to do, since we had never been abused before. The First Ones knew that they could never fight your people and win. Instead, they left, retreating to the Saw Tooth Mountains and later to Unicorn Valley.

"We trees, however, could not flee from your axes. I alone can change my shape—the other trees stand anchored where they were planted. We wanted to run away, but were trapped. So we fought back."

"What do you mean you fought back?" asked Luke incredulously. "How can a tree fight?"

"In those days," continued Alysia, "your people let their children run wild while they built their kingdom. Seeing your people's children made me think of my own babies that your people turned into timber.

"Day after day, I thought about it until I could think of nothing else: Your people did not deserve children. You chopped down the trees that I loved. You deserved to suffer the way you made me suffer. So one day, the surviving trees and I took all the children that came within reach, as restitution for the trees you chopped down."

"I heard about that," said Luke. "The trees slaughtered all the children of that first generation of settlers."

"We did not kill those children," the queen replied. "We kept them as replacements for our own lost children. Before long, they came to see our side of the story. They no longer wanted to go home. The forest became their home. We trees became their family."

"But what about their parents?" Luke asked. "Have you no idea how much pain you caused them? They all thought their children had been killed."

"And what of it?" Alysia snapped. "What about the pain they caused us? They really did kill our children—and for firewood!

"We never hurt their babies. In fact, we gave them immortality. Those children are the same faeries you see about you, frozen at whatever age they entered our forest."

Luke looked around. Alysia was the only adult at the table. The rest of the dinner guests were children. Some looked no older than two, while the eldest was perhaps fourteen.

Despite their queen's rich robes, most of the faeries wore ragged, piecemeal clothing. Their hair was tangled. Their feet were bare. The children had a wild, untamed look on their faces. Luke was not sure whether he felt sorry for the faeries or envied them.

Alysia seemed to grow taller and more imposing, commanding Luke's attention once more. She cleared her throat.

"We continued our *unconventional* war against the invaders until they finally begged for a truce," said Alysia. "They agreed to come no further south than the Old Highway and we agreed not to steal their children, unless—"

"Unless what?" asked the prince slowly.

"Unless their children should come into our territory," the faery queen replied. "They chop down our trees north of the Highway, and we keep their children who venture into our realm."

Luke thought about himself and his sister. He wondered if they could be ransomed or rescued. He realized the idea was ridiculous.

His father would have paid any ransom, but now he was dead. Their mother still lived, but she had been won over or enchanted by Count Damien. Meanwhile, the rest of the kingdom thought they were murderers.

No one was coming to save them. They would be prisoners in the Wranglands forever. Luke crossed his fingers and decided to bluff.

"Surely you know that my father's men will be looking for me," said the prince.

The queen responded coldly, "You prefer the death they would bring you to living here?"

Luke burned with anger against the queen, for knowing everything and for mocking him. He looked away from her cool blue eyes and glared instead at the candle centerpiece. The candles seemed to pulsate. Luke felt such hatred toward Alysia that he wished he could burn down the whole forest just to spite her—and then he exploded.

"You venomous toad! You miserable excuse for a—" roared Luke, knocking down the burning candles.

He forgot that his arms were—or were supposed to be—shackled to his chair. In an instant, the decorative wheat caught fire. Flames whipped up and down the table, sending everyone—even Alysia—into confusion.

CHAPTER **XII**
LEAVING THE TABLE

ꢝꢝꢝꢝꢝꢝꢝꢝꢝꢝꢝꢝ

The next moment, a fury of shrieks and chaos filled the air. Luke looked for the queen, but she had already disappeared from her seat. He looked down at his lap and saw that his iron shackles had vanished.

Luke slid under the table and shuffled toward where he had last seen his sister. He recognized her legs under the table—few banqueters still sat in their chairs and she was the only one wearing shoes.

"Lex! Lex! Get down here!" the prince whispered loudly to her. She bent her head down to look at him. She seemed oddly calm, as if she were in shock.

"I can't," she protested. "My legs are bound to the chair."

"No, they are not! It was all in your head!" Luke insisted. "Just get down here before the queen comes back!"

When Lexi looked down at her legs, she was surprised to find that the shackles had disappeared. Confused and disoriented, she obeyed her brother. Soon she crouched beneath the table beside him.

"So where is Megan?" asked Lexi.

"I came to you first," Luke replied. "I haven't rescued her yet."

A voice came from behind the prince.

"Who says I needed rescuing anyway?" asked Megan, grinning.

"Excellent!" Luke exclaimed.

"I don't know how comfortable you two are, but I'd like get out of here," Megan said. "I think our diversion is winding down out there."

The children looked up and down both lengths of the table. It was just as long underneath as it was above. They could dart out from underneath the table and make a break for the trees, but it seemed safer to stay sheltered from sight.

"Does either of you have any idea which way is which?" asked Lexi, weighing which direction they should go—up or down the length of the table.

"Not the slightest," said Luke.

"That's one of their tricks," Megan said knowingly. "Besides, it doesn't matter which way we go. This table never ends. It circles back on itself eventually."

"How would you know?" Lexi scowled. "It looks perfectly straight to me."

"I've heard a lot of faery stories," said Megan. "Appearances can be deceiving here in the Wranglands. Besides, if this table had a head and a foot, don't you think that the queen would sit at its head instead of along its side?"

"So we have to make a break for the forest to escape?" asked Luke.

"We also want to make sure we're heading back into the forest, out of this faery ring," said Megan. "While we're within the circle, we're almost certain to get caught. Once we're back in the forest we might actually get away."

Lexi thought for a minute. "It looks grassier on that side of the table," she said, pointing.

"I think you are right, Sis," said Luke.

"We have to hide on the forested side," said Megan. "That way we're actually on the outside of the faery circle and will be harder for them to catch."

"Okay," the twins chorused.

They looked out from their hiding place, past the elegant claw chair legs, to the safety of the shadows. The children could hear the faeries making merry again. The faery children's bare feet again hung down from nearly every seat.

Luke, Lexi and Megan all silently hoped that they had been forgotten in the shuffle. Even if they had not, they knew their only hope was to make a break for the trees. The three children edged toward a gap between two ornate chairs.

"Should we count down from three?" Lexi whispered.

"Just go!" Megan hissed, pushing Lexi forward.

The three scrambled for the woody refuge. The forest had seemed only a few feet away, but no matter how fast they ran, the trees never got any closer. With every step they took, the distance to the grove of trees stretched out more and more.

As the forest slipped further and further away, Lexi saw two yellow eyes flash at her from the distant trees. Birds and little forest creatures were free to come and go, but she felt sure she would be a prisoner forever.

"You are very rude guests—that is all I can say," called a voice from behind them. Against their will, they found themselves turning toward Queen Alysia.

Lexi looked at her brother and at Megan. They looked just as scared as she felt.

"I daresay, after a few decades, you will remember this day differently," said Alysia slowly. "You will wonder why you ever tried to escape the home that you love so much.

"I have claimed you. Now you belong to me and to my forest. Until the end of time, you will remain here as my guests, as my children." Alysia took a deep breath. "*That* is certain."

Lexi looked around. They were now completely encircled by faeries. The enchanted children would have looked like beggars had it not been for their gossamer wings.

At the table, Lexi had not seen the faeries' wings, but now she could not help but notice them.

Each faery's wings split every sunbeam into a thousand rainbows.

Her eyes could not look away from those wings. Everywhere she looked there was another faery, another brilliant pair of butterfly—no, dragonfly wings. She felt tired and dizzy.

Maybe joining the faeries was not such a bad idea. After all, they would be safe from Count Damien. Lexi shook herself awake, as a small child tries to stave off sleep.

Instead of heavy eyelids, her very consciousness felt heavy with exhaustion. She watched her companions with dreamlike curiosity.

"You can't keep us here!" cried Megan. "These two have to save the kingdom! I have to go home to my family!"

"Kingdoms and dynasties come and go," replied the queen. "Why should I care who occupies the throne, as long as the pompous fool leaves me alone?

"This is the first time, however, I have had an opportunity to add a prince and princess to my collection. Surely, you must understand."

"You're sick!" Megan spat. Luke put his arm around Megan and gave her a supportive squeeze. He stepped forward toward Alysia.

"As rightful king of this land, I command you to let us go!" Luke thundered, drawing his sword.

The queen laughed. "You have spoilt a marvelous banquet," she said with a smirk, "but another is being prepared in its place." Suddenly, catching sight of something beyond the prince, she blanched.

Lexi saw the huge, ferocious wolf behind Luke. For one very long moment, she thought that the bristling, snarling beast was a monster about to attack her brother. Then she realized that it was Wolfram.

Chapter XIII
LEXI'S TEMPTATION

ଉ୧୦ʄ˚ꙍଥꙛ୮ଡ଼ଉ୲ଌୱ୧୧ʑ୮ୱ˚୨ୢୣ୨୨,

"Alysia!" roared Wolfram. "Is this what you call hospitality?"

"Why, it looks like another of my little ones!" the queen smiled wryly. "I see I never taught you manners as well as I should have. What a shame . . . You were such a cute puppy, but you are not so cute anymore."

"The children are coming with me," said the wolf. "It is not right to keep them here."

"What is not right is you taking them out of the safety of this forest to certain death," Alysia said.

Although she spoke to Wolfram, her words seemed directed at Luke, Megan and Lexi.

"You know that Count Damien's men patrol the roads looking for them," the faery queen continued. "You know that he will see you all hanged when he catches you—and he *will* catch you. They have no chance outside my forest, but here they will be safe."

Wolfram looked right at Lexi, then at her brother and Megan.

"All of you, come with me," he said firmly. "We are leaving this place."

Megan and Luke flung a defiant glare at the faery queen before walking over to the giant wolf. Lexi, however, panicked.

She felt torn: Of course she wanted to be with her brother, but what if Alysia was right? What if they had no chance at all? She was frozen.

Seeing Lexi's hesitation, Alysia pounced. "You need not go with them, dear child. If they intend to get themselves killed, there is nothing you can do about that.

"Let them go. Stay here with us," she said smoothly. "We will laugh and make merry and shut out that ugly world of yours. I can offer you eternal peace. They can promise you only discomfort and death."

Lexi's eyes lingered on the beautiful gossamer wings that all the faeries wore. It would not be so bad to be a faery. She would have no cares and would be safe from worry. She would be safe from death itself. She would be free.

More than anything else, Lexi found herself wanting to submit to Alysia's powerful will. It would be such a relief to just give in. She felt so very tired.

"Wake up, Lexi!" cried her brother. "The queen's words are poison! Alysia does not care if Count Damien steals our kingdom and marries our mother! Alysia just wants to own you, as if you were some sort of trophy!"

Lexi thought of her mother. The princess' stomach turned. Despite her mother's strange behavior lately, Lexi loved her mother and could not bear to see her marry that scoundrel, Count Damien.

The queasiness in her belly seemed to wake Lexi up. Yes, a part of her did want to stay in the forest, free from cares and worries.

She realized that there would still be plenty to worry about if she stayed, only she would be too indifferent to care. Lexi looked up at Megan and at her brother's clear, blue eyes. She looked at Wolfram, whose worried expression made him seem more like a dog than the fearsome wolf he was.

Finally, Lexi walked toward her companions. Once she reached them, she found herself being hugged and squeezed and her face being licked by a very wet tongue.

"Stupid girl!" Alysia spat. She turned away. In a few minutes, all the winged children had gone and the forest was quiet again.

"Come on," said Wolfram. "We have a long way to travel before nightfall. Let's go."

* * *

"What happened back there?" Lexi asked Wolfram later on.

"You were tired and the queen saw that you were vulnerable," Wolfram answered. "A good hunter goes after the easy prey—the young, the old, the weak."

"But I am older than Luke, if only by a few minutes. I am older than Megan too."

"It is not your age that made you weak," said Wolfram. "She saw that you have doubts about our mission . . ."

Lexi opened her mouth to say something, but Wolfram continued, ". . . that you are unsure if we will survive. Alysia simply twisted your own fears around to manipulate you. Now stop worrying. We got away."

Luke, whose interest had been sparked, joined in. "Why did Alysia let us go, when she could have just made us stay?" he asked. "She seems to have all sorts of magical powers, but she tried to seduce us instead of just using force."

Wolfram walked on in silence for a few minutes. Luke wondered if the wolf had heard him. Finally, Wolfram spoke, "The queen *could* just make you stay in her domain, but that is not how she works.

This is a game to her. She does not want to own your body but your mind, your very being. Even if she held you prisoner, she would not really own you."

"But she did hold us as her prisoners," Lexi corrected. "She shackled us to our chairs at the banquet table."

"So if you were chained down, how did you escape?" asked Wolfram.

Luke looked up. By the look on his face, it was clear that something had clicked. "She was using magic to bind us," he said, "but it was just an illusion!"

"I couldn't move, though," Lexi insisted. "The iron was cold against my skin. I remember."

"You saw what she wanted you to see. You felt what she wanted you to feel," Wolfram continued. "Alysia is a very powerful sorceress.

"Instead of simply overpowering you by force, she made you believe that you could not escape. Then, when you realized that you could get away, she planted seeds of doubt in your mind about whether freedom was worth having."

"I am glad we got away from her," said Lexi. "Are you sure we are safe while still in her forest?"

"She will not bother us again," said Wolfram confidently.

Megan, who had walked silently since they left the faeries, finally spoke up. "So where's Depper?" she asked. She had not seen the horse since falling asleep in the faery ring.

After a long pause, Wolfram replied, "She spooked after you were taken. I am hoping she will catch up to us soon."

"And if she does not?" asked Lexi.

"Then we walk the rest of the way to the tunnels," Wolfram answered in a low growl.

* * *

Luke found himself remembering Queen Alysia as they walked. The faery queen's face haunted him. Although Luke understood that stealing children had been a part of the old war between the trees and man, it seemed so foreign and strange.

Every boy or girl taken had been a replacement for a lost tree, but now that war was over. Now Alysia keep on abducting stray children just to keep the people of Nèra Toli afraid of the forest. It seemed so unnecessary and heartless.

"It is already getting dark," Lexi observed, waking Luke from his thoughts. "When are we going to stop for dinner?"

"Soon," Wolfram answered.

Luke wondered how Wolfram had become their leader. *It's just as well,* he thought. Neither his sister nor he knew the way through the forest. *Someone* had to be their guide.

First, it had been John Boy, then Megan had guided them through the forest, and now their leader was a big, shaggy dog. Luke did not really like the idea of being the leader, himself, so it was a relief to be spared the worry for a little while.

Even though Megan and Wolfram might help them, Luke knew that he and his sister would be the ones to avenge their father's murder.

They would face Count Damien alone. Luke doubted that they would come out of this ordeal alive, but they had to confront Count Damien anyway. He could not run and hide for the rest of his life.

While Luke did not look forward to assuming his role as king, it was his duty. It would be selfish to leave the people of Nèra Toli in the hands of a treacherous ruler like Count Damien.

"We stop here for the night," Wolfram finally announced, stopping abruptly.

Luke looked around. A broad river stretched out before them. The sun had already set and everything took on a gray, dusky quality. Luke lapsed into his thoughts, while Megan built a fire.

Wolfram returned with game, which Megan soon skinned, gutted and skewered. She handed the prince and princess each a long stick, on which was skewered their share. They roasted their meat in silence for a long time.

"What is this, anyway?" asked Lexi, examining the meat on her skewer.

"Dinner," said Megan.

"You know what I mean," Lexi said. "What was it when it was alive?"

"A beaver," replied Megan, already scraping the hide.

"But beavers are so cute with their big, flat tails and their cute little faces," Lexi protested. "I can't eat a furry little beaver."

Megan sighed in exasperation. "If you aren't hungry, I'm sure the rest of us would be happy to eat your share," she suggested.

"Never mind," said Lexi, as her belly rumbled. "I will eat it." She doubted she could bear eating any more apples, which were the only alternative.

They all ate in silence. Then, one by one, they each lay down in front of the fire. As Luke closed his eyes, he could hear a wolf howling in the distance.

He sleepily hoped that Wolfram would protect them from the strange wolf. As he drifted off to sleep, he realized that it was Wolfram who was howling.

Lexi lay awake, longing for her goose feather bed. Only a few days ago she ate whatever was served without thinking about what her dinner had been when it was alive. She longed for those carefree days again.

She suspected, however, that her life would never be the same, even if things eventually got back to normal. She tossed and turned, trying to block out Wolfram's mournful howl.

Chapter XIV
ANOTHER DWARF

The next thing Luke knew, he felt something big and wet against his face. Blinking drowsily, he realized that the slobbery something was a large mouth. When the gigantic beast above him neighed, Luke recognized Depper immediately. He sat up and pushed down his bedroll. He rubbed Depper's great velvet nose and looked around.

Lexi still slept soundly, but Wolfram was nowhere to be seen. Megan, in contrast, had clearly been up for a while. She had already built a fire and sat frying freshly caught trout.

"Is breakfast ready?" said an unfamiliar voice. Luke looked around again, but saw no one. "Up here," the voice continued.

Luke looked up and saw a tiny person astride the behemoth horse, silhouetted against the morning sun. "Who are *you*?" he asked in surprise.

The little man dismounted, landing lightly on the ground. He bowed with a flourish, saying, "Roland Short at your service, Your Highness."

The prince tried not to stare at the newcomer, who was very clearly a dwarf. Roland's sunburnt face and brown eyes smiled broadly. His dark hair carried a hint of auburn, just enough to remind Luke of Megan.

Luke remembered Megan's diminutive parents and realized that this must be her brother. The prince did not know what to say, but knew he had to say something. This was Megan's kinsman, even if he was a dwarf. "Pleased to meet you," Luke said awkwardly.

"So how is my favorite sister doing?" Roland said, turning to Megan.

"I'm your *only* sister," she smiled. "Things could be better, but as you can see, we've made it this far."

"I'm impressed," said Roland. "You have half the palace guard on your heels. I see your friends even eluded Alysia."

"What can I say? I'm *that* good," Megan said casually, winking at Roland.

"Meg, I need to tell you something," said Roland, serious once more. His face had more lines than it had a moment earlier. Megan stopped smiling.

"What happened?" she asked quietly.

"They got Mom and Dad," said Roland. "I stopped by the cabin on my way to the castle, but when I got there the windows were broken and the front door .was open. There were a couple of drunken soldiers asleep on the porch. I didn't wait for them to wake up."

"Are Mom and Dad all right?" Megan asked, looking very pale.

"I don't know," replied Roland. "But I'll need your help to save them, if it's not already too late. Plus, I'm worried about you getting yourself mixed up with these two fugitives." He glanced at the prince and princess.

"How did you know where to find us?" asked Luke suspiciously.

"Alysia filled me in," Roland shrugged.

"That witch helped you?" Luke said in disbelief.

"She's a little eccentric, but once you get to know her she can be a useful ally," Megan responded defensively.

"I have a hard time believing that she could possibly be on our side," said Luke. "She held us captive."

"Believe it," said Roland. "She's the reason I found you. Her faeries have been tracking you since you left her. They led me right to you."

Luke said nothing, but looked unconvinced.

"Let's just say that she makes a better friend than an enemy," said Megan.

Just then, Lexi, who had been sleeping, awoke with a snort. "What smells so good?" she yawned, stretching. She opened her eyes, found herself face to face with the grinning horse and shrieked.

"It's only Depper," laughed Luke.

Lexi grumpily pushed the horse's great muzzle away. A moment later she said, "Wait a minute, who found Depper?"

"I did," said Roland. "She was wandering around in the forest."

"Who exactly are you?" asked Lexi, suddenly self-conscious about her messy hair and unwashed face.

"I'm Roland, Megan's brother," the little man grinned. "I take it you're that royal assassin all those armed men are looking for."

This newcomer was far too confident for a dwarf. He was charming and gregarious, but as a dwarf, it was not his place to be likeable. Lexi felt conflicted about this stranger.

On one hand, something about his eyes and smile drew her to him. On the other hand, nothing would change the fact that he was a dwarf. *He* was an untouchable. *She* was a princess.

"Megan, please tell your brother to go away if he refuses to treat his superiors respectfully," said Lexi indignantly, just to put Roland in his place.

Megan looked helplessly at her brother.

"I don't think my sister would be helping you if you really had killed the king," Roland continued, ignoring Lexi's rudeness. "Besides, now they're after me too."

103

"What do you mean?" asked Luke, his interest piqued.

"Those men at my parents' house didn't look like they would have been very friendly had they seen me," said Roland. "Since they think that even our parents are accomplices, I'm sure that makes Megan and me fugitives, too."

Lexi's irritation with Roland evaporated, but she avoided looking in his direction over breakfast. She felt embarrassed at insulting him, but was too proud to apologize. After breakfast, while everyone helped pack up camp, she finally spoke to him.

"So how long will you help us?" she asked.

"Until we can get our parents free," Roland replied, "or until they kill us."

"So are you are coming with us, then?" asked Lexi. "Megan talked about going through some tunnels under the mountains."

"Of course I'm coming," said Roland. "Who do you think is leading you?"

* * *

Wolfram returned just as Megan was dowsing the campfire. Lexi, Luke and Roland all stood around, ready to go.

"I have scouted out the area and we are still a bit ahead of Count Damien's men," said Wolfram. "If we follow the river, we should reach the base of the trail to the High Pass by nightfall."

At that, the party set off. Luke and Megan rode Depper while Wolfram carried Lexi and Roland. All the bedrolls and gear were also strapped to Depper, who scarcely could have carried her burdens were she not such a giant.

As they continued on their journey, Lexi felt grateful that Megan was there to show them the way. Megan led them along paths that they never would have been able to find on her own.

The trees and bushes seemed to part to let them through, closing again behind them. Sunlight streamed through the trees from above. But even with the sunbeams dancing around her, Lexi still thought there were too many shadows about.

The forest was friendly and welcoming, but she sensed that it could pour out its wrath upon them if it so desired. Lexi remembered the faery queen Alysia, who ruled these trees.

Despite their escape from her, Alysia had not chased after them or turned the trees unfriendly. The memory of the strange faery queen puzzled the princess, who disliked things she could not understand. Finally, Lexi's thoughts returned to the path and to Roland, who rode in front of her.

"Are you sure you are strong enough to carry both of us?" she asked Wolfram.

"Yes," he laughed. "I am as large as a small pony and far stronger than one. Besides, the two of you barely add up to the weight of an average-sized man."

"I'm not that small," Roland quipped indignantly.

"Well, you are not that large either," said Wolfram. "As for you, Lexi, it would be easy to forget that you're even there at all. You *are* still there, Lexi? Right?" The wolf laughed.

* * *

By noon, all were hot and hungry, so they rested in a shady spot by the river. Megan went off

105

to look for food and reappeared with ripe melons. The wayfarers split the fruit open and quickly devoured it. Wiping the sticky juice from his face, Prince Luke grinned at Megan.

"You're pretty useful to have around," he said. "Without you, we would be pretty hungry."

"I hope you know that I'm good for more than providing food," Megan responded with a sharp glance. "On the other side of the mountains, girls are valued for their intelligence and wisdom!"

"Of course," Luke cleared his throat. "I never said otherwise."

"But on this journey, the only thing you notice about me is when I cook for you or find you something to eat," Megan replied irritably. "I'm more than just some sidekick cook. If it weren't for me, you never would have gotten out of my parents' house. You'd still be being coddled by that John Boy of yours."

"He is not *my* John Boy," Luke was getting annoyed now. He had not meant to take Megan for granted. Her hostility perplexed him. "I was just trying to let you know that I appreciate you, but you claim I mean the very opposite."

"Let's go," said Megan, ignoring him. "If we hurry, we can make it to the caves by nightfall."

"Hey, I am the one in charge here!" said Luke, with a glance in Megan's direction. "It's time to go, so come on, everyone!"

* * *

Within a few minutes, they were again following the nearly invisible trail. No one said much of anything for a long time. Lexi could not understand what had gotten into her brother.

Suddenly, he seemed more eager to assert himself as the leader of the expedition, where he had hesitated before. The silence seemed unbearable. Finally, Roland spoke.

"Lexi," he said, "I understand that you are older than your brother, yet he is the one who will inherit the throne. Why is that?"

"Ask him yourself!" Lexi snapped. Megan's bad mood had rubbed off on her.

"I did not mean to offend you, Your Highness," said Roland. "I apologize if I did so. I hope that you will treat me as respectfully as I treat you."

Lexi looked away, feeling self-conscious. "Please forgive me," she said. "It is a sore subject with me. I lost my birthright because I am a girl. That is why I will never be queen."

"But why?" persisted Roland.

"Because I am a girl," said Lexi, "and only men can inherit the crown here in Nèra Toli. Didn't you know?"

"No," replied Roland. "Actually, I grew up rather isolated out here in the Wranglands. Mum and Dad chose not to live in a town because, as dwarves, we would have been outcasts."

"Oh," said Lexi.

"Why can't women rule?" asked Roland.

"My great-great-grandfather hated his mother and issued an edict saying that no woman should ever occupy the throne of Nèra Toli," said Lexi. "I suppose he thought his mum was a snake and wanted to punish all women for the fact that she was rotten."

"Well, I wouldn't worry," said Roland stoically. "It might not seem like it now, but you're actually quite fortunate not to be the future monarch. It's a terrible burden. I wouldn't be king for all the riches in Nėra Toli."

It bothered Lexi that Roland could so easily dismiss what she would do almost anything to have.

"Of course you could never be king," she retorted. "No one of dwarf blood can ever inherit the throne, especially not an actual dwarf!"

Roland turned very red. He opened his mouth to speak, but thought better of it and said nothing. Lexi regretted her words instantly.

She knew she should apologize, but could not bring herself to admit that she had been wrong. Wolfram carried the two onward and an uneasy silence loomed between them.

CHAPTER XV
AN IMPOSSIBLE PROPOSAL

ᒉᘓᘎᓍᕼᕋᕋᕼᓍᕋᘎᘓᒉ

A few paces ahead, Megan and Luke sat astride Depper. They were in the midst of their own conversation.

"So once we reach your tutor, this Timothy fellow, what's your plan?" Megan asked.

"I will seek his aid in avenging my father's murder," Luke said solemnly. "Then I will unseat this Count Damien and see him brought to justice."

"But why the big hurry?" asked Megan. "If he takes over Nèra Toli, you'll know where he is. You can hunt him down anytime."

"He is about to marry my mother and crown himself king," Luke protested. "I can't stand by and let him dishonor her."

Megan twisted to face Luke and said, "If my mother were about to marry my father's killer, *her* welfare would be the least of my worries. It seems to me that she must have been involved in Count Damien's plot."

"I refuse to believe *that*," Luke denied flatly. "I know my own mother."

"Lexi told me that your mum has been acting strangely for months now," said Megan. "I bet she has joined Count Damien's side. Anyway, I wouldn't risk my life just to get revenge. I certainly wouldn't bother trying to rescue someone who set me up for a crime that she helped commit."

"What do you propose I should do?" asked Luke.

"Flee," said Megan. "If I were you, I would keep going west from Miriam's cave all the way to the Western Sea."

"But what about your parents?" Luke asked incredulously. "You would just leave them in Count Damien's hands to be tortured?"

"I said that's what I would do if I were *you*," said Megan. "Honestly, I think Roland and I would be better off trying to rescue our parents without your help.

"You two attract too much attention, since everyone knows what you look like. You should lay low for a while with Timothy and Miriam, then start a new life in exile."

"I refuse to believe you would just let Count Damien win like that," said Luke. "He is obviously a monster. How can I just let him take over Nėra Toli without a fight?"

"The way I see things, you're not that different from him," Megan replied coldly. "If you become king, nothing will really change.

"You'll continue your silly feud with the trees. You'll keep treating dwarves as if they're subhuman. You'll be no different from all the rest of the kings of Nėra Toli who came before you."

"Do you honestly believe that, just because Alysia tried to trap us, I am going to be an enemy to the Wranglands?" said Luke. "As for the dwarf laws, you are not even a dwarf, so why should you care?" Luke asked.

"In case you haven't noticed, I'm dwarf-born," said Megan. "To lead a normal life in Nėra Toli, I'd have to live a lie. I'd have to disown my heritage and pretend to have no family.

"Why do you think that my parents and I live in the wilderness the way we do? Alysia and her faeries may have their faults, but at least they don't judge me just because my parents are small."

"I didn't mean it that way," Luke stammered. "So your parents are dwarves. Who cares?"

Megan's expression softened, but she said nothing. Luke continued, "I like you just the way you are, and back when I said I liked your cooking, I meant it with the deepest respect."

"I like you too, but you know marriage is not an option," said Megan pointedly. "Your own laws forbid intermarriage between royalty and those with dwarf blood."

"That is not what I meant," said Luke defensively.

For a while, neither said anything. Finally, Megan said, "I would join you in exile, you know."

"Say again?" asked Luke.

"If you kept going once we reach Miriam's cave," said Megan. "I'd meet you after rescuing my parents. We could go anywhere."

"I thought you said I am not that different from Count Damien," said Luke. "What would you want to marry me for? Besides, it is ridiculous to even talk like this. We only just met and I am already engaged to someone else."

"So you'd rather spend your life with some girl you've never met?" Megan asked.

"How should I know?" Luke sighed. "Royal marriages have always been arranged. What do we know about what is best for us, anyway?"

"Brides are not chattel to be purchased by the highest bidder," said Megan. "I am glad my parents love me enough not to sell me through a bride broker."

"So where would we go if you came with me?" Luke asked curiously.

"Across the mountains, to the south, there is a land where dwarves rule. It is a fat country and we would prosper there. There are also the People of the Arrow, who live in Unicorn Valley, between the mountains.

"They might let us live in their protection," said Megan. "Then again, it still isn't too late to go back to the Wranglands and dwell among Alysia's faeries and the living trees."

A moment later, Depper reared as something darted out in front of her. It was a young boy of perhaps ten years old. Like the other faeries they had seen, he wore ragged, mossy garments.

"I have been tracking you since you left my Mistress. She bade me to repeat her invitation," the boy said.

"She offers you her protection, this time without conditions," he continued. "You may leave her country whenever you so wish, if indeed you should ever wish to return to your own unpleasant world."

Luke looked at the child before him. For a long moment, he felt tempted to stay in the protection of the Faery queen, but he imagined his father lying dead and cold somewhere in the castle.

More than ever, Luke wanted to make Count Damien pay for what he had done. He would never rest until he brought Count Damien to justice.

"I bid you thank Alysia for her hospitality, but I must decline her offer," said Luke. "When I next visit her house, I will do so as king of Nėra Toli."

"Very well, Your Highness," said the young messenger. "Good fortune to you in your quest. May our next meeting find you alive and victorious."

A moment later, Lexi called ahead to her brother, "Luke! Who was that little elf you were talking to?"

"Just another messenger from that witch Alysia," Luke replied.

"It is unlucky to speak ill of the fair folk," Wolfram scolded.

"Who asked you?" Luke snapped. "She raised you, after all, so of course you would side with her. Besides, you are just a—"

"I must beg Your Highness not to slander the good Queen Alysia or her friends if you would have us survive long enough to avenge your father," Roland added. "We are but a stone's throw from the entrance to the caves, but we are not there yet."

"How far do we have to go?" asked Lexi, changing the subject.

"Not far," Roland said, fingering his crossbow nervously.

Just then, a whizzing sound interrupted them. "Ouch! Something stung me!" exclaimed Lexi, wiping her cheek. When she looked at her hand, there was blood on it. Turning around, she saw an arrow planted in the trunk of the tree behind her. It had only grazed her.

"Take cover!" shouted Luke, as a half-dozen more arrows whizzed around them. "That blasted witch has ambushed us!"

Depper reared and whinnied before darting forward. Luke and Megan clung to the giant horse's back as Depper broke into a gallop. Wolfram growled to his charges, "Hold on! We don't want to lose them."

The next instant, he charged forward while Roland and Lexi held on for dear life. Lexi could not see the trail at all now, just one tree after another appearing to dash out of their way as they sped onward. As she clung to Wolfram's fur, Lexi noticed the smell of water.

The next few minutes were a blur as the twins and their companions found themselves tossed around like so many sacks of potatoes. Then Lexi suddenly felt herself flying through the air, falling headlong into chilly water.

She struggled to the surface, gasped for air and saw Roland beside her in the brisk water. Lexi could not see her brother, Megan or Wolfram anywhere. Then, out of nowhere, Luke dove into the water followed by a shower of arrows.

"Get down!" Roland ordered, dunking Luke and Lexi.

Lexi swam underwater as far as she could from the raining arrows, before her lungs felt like they were going to burst. She finally surfaced for a breath. She saw her brother and Roland nearby.

"Use this to breathe," Roland said, tossing a hollow reed to each of the twins. "Quick! Get down!"

Lexi ducked underwater, sticking the straw up to the surface. Her first breath brought water into her lungs.

She rose, coughing, above the surface of the water, only to be yanked down again by Roland. He motioned to her to plug her nose while breathing in through the reed. She tried again and got air.

Opening her eyes underwater, Lexi wondered where they were. The sun had already set, so she could see little through the dusky water. She could still touch the ground, since Roland herded the twins near the grasses by the banks.

Eventually, Roland motioned to the twins to surface. From where they were behind large patches of reeds, they could just barely see a dozen armed men on the distant shore.

Lexi noticed some commotion beside the armed men. There she saw three men rolling around on the ground, fighting a furious ball of teeth and claws.

A moment later, she saw a flash of copper hair amid the men: It was Megan they were wrestling.

Chapter XVI
A WALK IN THE DARK

ꭹꭉꮓꭼ ꭼꭱꭹ ꭺꮩꮿ ꮙꮅꭼ ꭼꮧ

From where they hid, Luke, Lexi and Roland watched the struggle on the other side of the water. Finally, the three burly men pinned the slight—but furious—girl at the water's edge.

"Swine!" Megan yelled, thrashing against her captors.

"Just you wait until we find the rest of your friends, you dwarf-born trash!" said the stoutest of her captors, boxing her ears.

Megan spat in the guard's face. His next blow knocked her to the ground.

117

"Hanging may be too good for you and your friends. Maybe we'll have ourselves a good, old-fashioned summer bonfire," the guard continued. "What do you think, Drake? This little vixen looks a bit like a witch to me . . ."

"She looks like a sorceress—or I'm a wizard!" the other guard laughed. "I'll bet she wouldn't even drown if we held her underwater."

The third guard grabbed Megan just below her jaw and moved her head toward the water. She renewed her struggle as the cold water soaked her hair and ears.

A man on horseback approached and barked, "Knock it off, you three!"

"Come on, we were just having a little fun with her," replied the second guard.

"Stop wasting time!" the captain said sternly. "It's bad enough that you let the prince and princess escape. We'll never find them in this light.

"I'll not have you throw away the one trophy we've found today. She's useless to us dead. Tie her up! Let's get out of here before that witch of the Wranglands notices us."

The portly guard laughed, "I never knew Captain Otto to be afraid of children's stories."

The captain gave the guard a wicked kick to the head. "Don't talk about things you don't understand, fool!" he shouted. "I'm in no mood to lose anyone on my watch, though *you* would be no great loss. Stay together! Those who get lost in these woods return without their minds."

"I fear no woman, witch or no!" the guard mumbled under his breath, rubbing the side of his head.

"Shut your mouth, before she hears you!" the captain snapped. "Besides, if the witch doesn't get you, the Wild Man of the Mountain will. He'll take more than your mind, that one will."

Luke, Lexi and Roland stared gaping as the soldiers bound Megan and secured her to Captain Otto's impatient horse. Luke's face betrayed his horror at losing Megan.

"I've got to do something," he murmured, rising. Lexi wondered if her brother had gone mad.

Lexi and Roland held Luke back with every ounce of their strength. Luke pushed his sister aside. She landed hard on the rocky shore. Roland, despite his small size, somehow kept Luke from passing.

Lexi was still sure Count Damien's henchmen would hear their splashing any minute. Feeling helpless, she nervously handled one of the thousands of small round stones at the water's edge.

She could just make out an egret night fishing nearby in the dusk. The graceful white bird stood out against the surrounding darkness. How she envied that levelheaded hunter. Lexi wished she were the hunter, rather than the hunted.

"If you care at all about my sister, do not throw away your life like this," Roland said gravely, his face inches from Luke's. "As long as you are not captured, she has a chance. Once they have you and your sister, Megan's life will be worth nothing to these monsters."

"Did you hear something over there?" the stout guard said, looking in their direction.

He splashed through the shallow water toward them, holding a torch out against the darkness. The flame cast a flickering yellow light on the surface of the water, illuminating the tall graceful egret.

Lexi still gripped a stone in her hand. Without thinking, she hurled the stone at the great white bird. It cried out sharply and took flight.

"Come, Bruno!" The captain called. "We don't have time for bird watching!"

The guard turned around and returned to his comrades. "That was no bird I heard," he grumbled under his breath.

"Listen to me," Lexi whispered her brother. "If you make any noise, they will find us for certain next time. I promise you we will save Megan, but you know as well as I do that we need a plan. We need help. We need to get to Timothy."

"But I can't leave her!" Luke protested. "How can I live with myself, knowing that I could have done something?"

"Would you rather *actually* help her, or just *feel* courageous?" Roland demanded.

"I want to *be* a hero, not just feel like one," Luke acquiesced.

"Good, then follow me," said Roland. "If we walk through the night and all day tomorrow, we should reach the Seer's cave by next nightfall. Even if your Timothy isn't there, Miriam will help us rescue my sister."

Once the guards and their captive disappeared into the darkness, the three fugitives finally ventured out of the water. They shivered in the evening chill, but dared not light a fire.

Finally, a gibbous moon rose, and they could see to move about. Lexi's stomach rumbled. Oh what she would do for even a sandwich, an apple, even a potato!

Her heart dropped when she realized that all the food was in the saddlebags. The packs had been strapped to Depper, who had disappeared along with Wolfram in the ambush!

"Roland," Lexi began, "please tell me you have an idea about what we could have for dinner."

"How can you think about food at a time like this?" Luke demanded.

"It is too late to hunt or fish for dinner," said Roland, "and even if we did catch anything we dare not light a fire to cook it."

"So we are just supposed to starve for the next day-and-a-half, while walking nonstop," Lexi muttered under her breath, still shivering and wet.

"Fortunately," continued Roland, "there happens to be a hot meal in our future."

"What do you mean?" asked Luke.

"The caves under the mountain," Roland said. "Remember?"

"Before the ambush, you said we were close," Lexi said excitedly. "How far do we have to go?"

"Follow me," smiled Roland, "We'll eat within the hour."

* * *

Roland led the twins upstream along the water's edge toward the base of a tall waterfall. Before them, it seemed as if the very mountain rose out of the ground like an iceberg from the sea.

Down the face of the mountain came a torrent of water, but they could see little in the dark. Lexi reached for Roland and her brother as the waterfall's mist enveloped them.

"Now what?" asked Luke.

"Keep walking," answered Roland. "Everyone hold hands and follow the shore."

The three companions blindly walked through the mist. They walked single file in the narrow spots. Lexi's right foot felt numb from the cold water, while her left heel ached from the sharp little stones on the bank.

Her delicate slippers had long since crumbled to pieces. They had not been made for the heavy wear of a journey, but for lounging in the royal palace.

I'm not cut out for questing! Lexi thought to herself. Lexi had never realized before how much she had enjoyed being a princess. Only now that she had tasted the weary business of being on a quest did she appreciate the pampered life she had left behind.

As they walked onward, Lexi suddenly awoke from her self-pitying thoughts. The waterfall sounded different. She realized that it was now to her right instead of in front of her. They were behind the water. It was still misty and impossible to see anything, but she still felt Roland and Luke's hands in her own. To the left, she could see an opening in the rock.

They turned to go down the tunnel. Before long, the floor of the passageway was dry. Up ahead, light and shadows danced on the limestone walls. She rubbed her eyes, wondering if they were playing tricks on her. The tunnel widened into an enormous cavern, with a blazing fire at its center. He saw dark figures disappear into the shadows.

Chapter XVII
THE CATACOMBS OF ATSASH

ʃℋ§ᵕꝗℋℓℓᵕℂℤᵕℰℓℒℬℊʲᵕℰℒᵕℋℊʲᵕℂℚ

"What was that?" asked Luke, pointing where the figures had disappeared into the darkness.

"They are friendly, but very shy," returned Roland, sitting down in front of the fire. He removed the spit from where it had been roasting over the fire, helping himself to its aromatic meat.

"Are they coming back?" Lexi asked nervously. "Who are they anyway?"

"They are the Men of the Mountain," Roland answered, passing a drumstick to each twin. "I have shown them the art of fire, so I am always welcome

124

at their hearth. Even though I'm their friend, they are wary of other visitors. They will come back when we leave."

"I have heard of the Mountain Men," Luke commented. "People say they are wild savages. People say that they attack all who enter their territory."

"Are you sure it is safe to take this route through their territory?" Lexi asked, having second thoughts.

"You are right to be cautious," Roland said. "The Men of the Mountain attack trespassers without asking questions, but they will not attack us. You travel under my protection, so they will not harm you."

"Megan said the same thing about Queen Alysia and look what happened," said Luke.

"What happened with Queen Alysia?" asked Roland. "It looks to me like she let you go. You're here aren't you?"

"You seem to be friends with all manner of unseemly characters," Lexi said. "You reassure us that we are safe, but how do we know we really are?"

"My friends are not evil. The Men of the Mountain are enemies only to those who think of *them* as enemies. Alysia is an enemy to those who wield axes in her forest. You have been taught that the Mountain Men and the Fair Folk hate you, which is false. They just want to be left alone.

They don't care to have their land trampled by your countrymen with land hunger. So they will fight your people one traveler at a time, but you are safe with me. The ancient custom of hospitality requires my friends to treat my guests with honor."

"Friends or no, I will be happier when we are no longer at their hearth," said Luke.

"Your Highness would be better off resting before we continue our journey. There will be nowhere else to rest until we reach the summit," said Roland.

"I agree with Luke," said Lexi. "I would rather not stay here any longer. I believe you when you say that the Mountain Men will let us pass. I just keep remembering the stories I have been told about them."

"All our lives, grown-ups have told us that, if we are bad, the wild men will come and devour us," said Luke. "I just want to get out of this place."

"As you desire," Roland acquiesced, getting to his feet. He packed a satchel with some food and a wineskin. He gathered a few new, unlit torches for the long, dark walk before them.

"I hope they don't think we are stealing these supplies," said Lexi. "Do you think they will?"

"No," replied Roland curtly. "I bring supplies for the Mountain Men in exchange for their hospitality when traveling through the mountain. They actually make these torches for me—they don't need torches for themselves."

"Oh," Lexi said, embarrassed. She reached for her cloak, which she had taken off in front of the fire. Picking it up, she felt something cold and scaly touch her hand.

Lexi screamed and a dark little snake slithered off into the shadows. The princess's shrill scream filled in the large cavern. Then came another scream and again another.

A moment later, the air was a flurry with shrieking and a thousand beating wings. The three travelers dove for cover as panic-stricken bats filled the air. Finally, several minutes later, the cavern was quiet again, except for an occasional bat flapping by.

"Was that really necessary, Your Highness?" asked Roland, with an affectionate twinkle in his eye.

"There was a snake," said Lexi defensively. "I hate snakes!"

"I daresay you like bats better," Roland replied playfully. At that, Lexi rolled her eyes.

"Enough squabbling, you two!" said Luke. "You are like an old married couple!" Roland and Lexi's eyes met and they both blushed.

"Let's get this over with," the prince continued, getting to his feet again.

The trio picked up their cloaks, the satchel and the spare torches. Lexi carried the lit torch while the boys split the rest of the burden.

"All right, follow me," Roland said, walking toward one of the many passageways branching out from the main cavern. "Lexi, if you are going to carry the torch, you will have to walk up front so that we can see where we are going."

"I thought you knew where you were going," retorted the princess.

"I *do* know where I'm going," said Roland. "I still need to be able to see, though, in case there's anything on the ground. You know—snakes, scorpions, spiders."

"Now you are just being mean," Lexi grumbled lightheartedly.

As they trod along, Lexi thought her brother looked more and more pensive. She could already see the burden of crown beginning to weigh upon his shoulders.

The party continued down the corridor. Sometimes the passageway was almost square in shape with roughly hewn walls. Other times, it joined what looked like a natural, preexisting network of tunnels. The ground beneath them was worn smooth, perhaps by thousands of unknown feet in centuries past.

One thing is certain, Luke thought. *These passageways were not carved by the hands of wild men.* He wondered what earlier, forgotten civilization had created these tunnels out of the stone.

Luke looked ahead at his sister and their dwarf companion. It pained him to know that she envied him for being heir to the throne. He wished he could just give his sister the crown she so desired. He certainly did not want it.

Being king would mean marrying a girl he had never met. As king, he could never be free to live his life as he desired.

How ironic! thought Luke. He had spent his entire life being groomed for a throne he was in no hurry to occupy. Luke remembered that princes become kings only because of their fathers' funerals. He wished he could have his father back for even one more day.

The prince remembered practicing falconry with his father. There were so many things that they would never do together anymore. There were all sorts of questions Luke wished he had asked his father when he still had the chance.

First, he reminded himself, he had to win back the crown from that treacherous Count Damien. Luke wondered how in Nėra Toli they were going to get back to the castle in time. They had already traveled so many miles. Every hour brought them further from where they wanted to be.

He hoped that Timothy, their wise tutor, would be able to help them. They did not even know for sure whether Timothy had even sought refuge at the summit of the mountain. It was only blind hope that they followed now.

"Oh, look at that!" came Lexi's awed voice.

Luke looked up, grateful for any distraction from his dark thoughts. The passageway had opened up into another large cavern.

These walls had not been cut by any human hands, but looked like drips of wet, shimmering sand. There were great columns of melted stone stretching above them. Lexi stood speechless for once.

"What are those?" asked Luke, pointing.

"The hanging icicles of rock are stalactites, and those rising from the floor are stalagmites," said Roland. "Welcome to the Catacombs of Atsash."

"I never knew there was anything so wonderful in the world!" Lexi stammered, awestruck.

"Few of your countrymen have seen the living stone," Roland said, "and few ever will."

Turning his eyes from the magnificent icicles of frozen stone above, Luke saw an expansive subterranean lake before them. Their small flame lit only a small corner of the lake, leaving long black shadows on its dark surface. The tunnel led directly to the water's edge. Luke saw no way around the expanse of water.

"Where do we go from here?" asked Lexi, with a hint of trepidation.

"I thought we would swim," Roland said with a twinkle in his eye.

"Ha, ha," Luke replied dryly.

"The boat is over there," Roland smiled, "behind that column."

Lexi, who still held the torch, illuminated the spot where Roland had gestured. There lay a long narrow boat whose front curved up and forward in a spiral. The light danced upon the delicate carved patterns on the boat's side.

Lexi wondered who could have made such a marvelous vessel. Surely Roland had not made it all by himself. The boat looked ancient, as if it were from some forgotten era.

The three travelers pushed the boat halfway into the water and got in, careful not to get wet. Luke and Lexi watched their guide in awed silence.

Roland did everything with exact precision, despite his short, awkward limbs. Instead of oars, Roland pulled out a long pole. He pushed away from shore and the boat glided across the subterranean lake.

"How far do we have to go?" Luke asked, breaking the silence.

"It'll take several hours to navigate the Catacombs before we reach to the stairs," answered Roland. "Then we'll have another day's trek before us."

"And then we will finally reach Timothy," added Lexi.

"If fortune favors us," Roland said forebodingly.

Neither twin asked what they would do if fortune did not favor them, or if Timothy was not with Miriam. They moved silently through the water.

"Why do you use those poles instead of oars?" Lexi eventually asked.

"It's best not to touch the water," answered Roland cryptically. "Besides, we'll be going through some passages that are barely as big as this boat. It's easier to propel off the walls of the cave with poles than with oars."

There was something about Roland's first comment that bothered Lexi. Why should they avoid touching the water?

She looked at the impenetrable glassy surface and realized that she did not even want to know what lurked beneath. In fact, she had a sudden and distinct desire *not* to uncover its secrets. The princess resolved not to ask Roland any more questions.

Luke, meanwhile, had been caught up in his own thoughts. He had absolutely no plan on how to win back his kingdom. He did not even know how he and his sister were going to clear their names.

Luke reminded himself that his subjects probably accepted Count Damien's lie that he and Lexi were their father's assassins. How were others to know that the evidence against the prince and princess was planted?

Maybe Megan was right; maybe they should just flee for their lives and let Count Damien have the throne he so coveted. Luke remembered Megan's face and knew that he could not abandon her or her diminutive parents to certain death.

"You spend more time thinking than any other teenagers I have ever met," Roland commented.

Luke blinked and Megan's face was gone again. "I have a lot on my mind," he said defensively. "You may not care about Megan, but I do."

"Hey, she's *my* sister. *You* only just met her," Roland snapped. "I don't know what you want with her anyway. You know the law: It is forbidden for the blood of the dwarf-born to contaminate the royal line. Do you want her for a mistress then? Why do you insult her honor with your affection?"

"You forget yourself, *dwarf!*" Luke said with all the spite he could muster. "You are talking to the rightful king of Nėra Toli, in case you forgot!"

Just then, a strange sound echoed through the caverns. Like a plague of locusts, thousands upon thousands of wings beat furiously through the darkness. Luke, Lexi and Roland suddenly found themselves surrounded by another swarm of bats.

As stray bats collided with her, Lexi waved her arms frantically and screamed in the darkness. Even Luke and Roland let out an occasional shriek. A moment later, the bats had disappeared again into the darkness whence they had come.

"Ugh," said Lexi.

"What is it, Sis?" asked Luke.

"Bat droppings . . ." said Lexi, scooping up water from the lake to wash off her soiled sleeve.

"Do not disturb the water!" Roland yelled, but it was too late.

Chapter XVIII
STAIRWAY TO SOMEWHERE

𝓇𝓉𝓞𝓊𝓬𝓞𝓞𝓵𝓇𝓈 𝓃𝓉 𝓉𝓞𝓊𝓬𝓇𝓇𝓔𝓉𝓈

A long, serpentine shape suddenly surfaced perhaps ten yards away from them. It moved closer until it glided along beside the boat in the water.

The prince and princess could not take their eyes off the strange creature. The serpent had a small ridge of fins along its spine. Its scales seemed to sparkle with their own light.

"Oh, good," said Lexi with relief. "It is swimming beside us the same way dolphins swim with Father's ships."

"I know it is madness," said Luke, "but I just want to go in the water and get a better look at this creature. I have a good feeling about it." He sounded bewitched.

"Do *not* get in the water!" Roland commanded. "Quick! Poke the beast with a pole!"

Lexi could not understand what Roland was talking about. Then the serpent disappeared again, but it still glowed faintly beneath the water's surface.

"Oh, it went away," said Lexi sorrowfully.

Suddenly, the scaly serpent leapt out of the water and clear over the boat. It dove into the water again, circled them and again leapt around the boat.

"Poke the beast!" Roland shouted in vain. "We have to get to the stairs!"

Luke saw what might be stairs rising straight out of the water a few dozen yards away. Coming to his senses, he grabbed one of Roland's long poles to ward off the serpent that gripped their boat.

Luke and Roland stabbed at the serpent, but to no avail. Luke thought that perhaps the beast would crush their boat to splinters, but instead it simply pulled the boat beneath the water. Water flowed over the prow and suddenly they were in the water. It was not as cold as the prince had been expecting.

He flailed in the direction of Lexi and Roland, but then the lantern got wet and all was darkness. All he could see was the glowing body of the serpent as it splashed around, seeking them.

Luke tried to orient himself toward where he remembered seeing the stairs before the light had disappeared. He felt hair in his fingers and heard his sister shriek.

He half-swam, half-splashed through the water, hauling his sister along with some otherworldly strength. Then, suddenly, his head struck stone. He scrambled up the angular stone slope, dragging Lexi by her hair. With his last ounce of strength, he hurled himself and his sister clear of the water.

From a safe distance, Luke looked back toward the subterranean lake. He could still see the glowing form of the serpent lurking and its great eyes as big as saucers, but he could not see Roland anywhere.

The prince's eyes searched the darkness for some sign of Roland and their boat, but in vain. Luke turned to his sister, who sat coughing up water.

"You saved my life," Lexi gasped when she could speak again.

"I just wish I could have saved Roland's," Luke said helplessly. "If I had not been fighting with him, those bats would not have flown over us and we would not have touched the water trying to wash off the guano."

"I was the one that touched the water, not you," said Lexi bitterly. "I would have been more careful if I had known what would happen. How are we ever going to get out of here without Roland?"

"He pointed us in the right direction before we were pulled into the water," said Luke. "If I am not mistaken, we are actually on the stairs right now."

They felt around in the darkness and indeed, it seemed almost too miraculous to be true—they were on stairs.

Of course, there could be countless stairways to who knows where, Luke thought. *Who cares where they go as long as they go up!*

By the edge of the sloping wall, icicles of stone rose from the floor. Luke remembered what Roland had said about how slowly stone grew in the Caverns, drip by drip. How many hundreds or thousands of years ago had these stairs been carved from the living stone?

The twins dared not walk up the wet stairs in the blackness. Instead, they crawled upward, keeping each other within arm's reach for fear of falling. Now they were truly alone, their guide claimed by the darkness below. How they yearned for light, any light.

Neither of them dared consider the possibility that they were going the wrong way, or that perhaps the stairs did not go anywhere at all. They both clung desperately to the hope that at the top of those stairs they would find Miriam waiting for them with a crackling fire, dry clothes and food.

Never before have a prince and princess of Nèra Toli gone so long without the simple comforts of life! Lexi silently lamented.

She longed for her sheltered past. It was ironic that she had felt unsuited for royal life: Now she yearned desperately for all the luxuries that had once seemed so tiresome.

Luke finally broke the silence. "We should rest here for a while. We have been climbing for hours, or at least, I think we have been."

"I will never be able to start again if we stop now," said Lexi.

"We have to take a break or we are going to die of exhaustion," Luke insisted.

Lexi did not like the idea of dying from exhaustion. She was getting too tired to argue. They rested in place draping themselves on the cold stone stairs.

"I figure we can rest for a few hours and then get going again," said Luke, but Lexi was already asleep. He lay his head down on the smooth, wet stone. He closed his eyes and for once was too tired to think.

* * *

Luke and Lexi both awoke with a start. They had heard something. They opened their eyes but saw only endless darkness.

"Let's get going again," Lexi suggested.

"Agreed," said Luke.

The prince and princess climbed the stairs as quickly as their stiff, aching bodies could carry them. They heard a shuffling behind them, down the tunnel coming from that horrible lake.

"Suppose it's Roland . . ." Lexi said after a time. She hoped with all her heart that Roland still lived. She wished she had told him how she felt about him when he had been with her.

"Suppose it is *not* him! Then what?" replied Luke. "We have no way to defend ourselves. We don't even have any light to see our attacker!"

"But what if it *is* him? What if he needs our help?" Lexi persisted.

The sound of footsteps continued to echo toward them in the blackness.

"Sis, I know you are fond of Roland, but there is no way we can go back for him," said Luke.

"I am not *fond* of Roland. He is a dwarf. I am a princess," Lexi said defensively. "I am just concerned for his well-being."

"Right . . ." said Luke doubtfully.

"It just feels like we have abandoned him down there," said Lexi.

"We have no way of knowing if he is still alive," Luke reminded her. "If Roland is the one following us, we can wait for him in the comfort of Miriam's house. We can do nothing for him here in this place."

They kept climbing onward and onward. Even though Lexi hoped with all her heart that it was Roland that they heard shuffling toward them from so far away, she climbed faster just in case it was some monster instead.

Lexi remembered how Roland had said they had a day's climb ahead of them. Had it been that long? They had rested, but how long ago had that been?

Without the sun to guide them, neither sibling had a real sense of the passage of time. It was all a terrible dream but they could never wake up. Suppose they were climbing the wrong stairs . . . Lexi wondered how much longer she could go on like this.

"Ouch!" Lexi said crossly. "Something just cut me!"

The stairs had been less moist for a while and now they had become downright jagged. In fact, the stairs had actually disappeared. The tunnel still went upward, but the slope was shallow.

There was earth in among the rocks now. After a little while, they started to see roots growing into the sides of the tunnel. It even seemed a little brighter ahead.

They had long since stopped crawling upward and started walking, but now both the prince and princess broke into a run, despite the darkness. They had even forgotten the shadowy follower behind them.

Lexi ran and ran, certain that they were nearly out the mountain. Luke scarcely dared imagine that they were nearly through their ordeal. But the tunnel seemed to be getting narrower and narrower.

Then he felt the hard packed earth against his head—the ceiling was definitely getting lower. The tunnel leveled out and curved slightly to the left. Then there was a stone door. The door stretched from the passageway's ceiling to floor and left to right.

Lexi kicked the door in exasperation. Luke ran at it with all his might, but only managed to bruise his shoulder.

"We are so close!" Lexi cried. "I refuse to give up!"

"That door is not moving," said Luke, "but maybe we can get around it. It is not all stone here, after all. Maybe we can dig our way out."

Both sides of the door were sealed tightly, but some light shone through from underneath. The twins could just make out their bare environment.

Luke pulled a jagged rock from the wall of the tunnel and began to dig at the earth beneath the door. Lexi joined him, resigning herself to even more dirt underneath her fingernails.

The prince and princess dug diligently, despite having nothing to eat or drink in goodness knows how long. Finally, the hole under the door was big enough for them to slide under, one at a time.

"I will go first," said Luke, "just in case there is anything dangerous out there."

"I am sure it is safer than in here," said Lexi, looking over her shoulder into the darkness.

As Luke was crawling under the door, Lexi heard a sound from the void. A voice echoed from the depths of the mountain. The princess thought she heard the thud of feet in the tunnel.

"Hurry up!" Lexi whispered urgently. "Something is coming!"

"I'm trying!" snapped Luke. "This hole is not big enough. I am stuck."

Again, Lexi heard the voice in the darkness, but she could not make out what it said. The tunnel muffled the words, but she did not want to wait around to hear them.

She shoved her brother until he was finally clear of the hole. Then she dove after him, terrified of the unknown creature that pursued them through the darkness.

When Lexi was halfway through the hole, Luke began pulling on her arms. She was going to make it! Then she shuddered to feel something cold touch her ankle. With one more yank, Luke pulled her to freedom, but the voice still followed after.

"Wait up, Lexi!" came a familiar voice through the door.

It was Roland.

Chapter XIX
A WARM BED

ℰℨℰ ⁓ℰℰⅉℐ℩⁓ℬℐℓℓ⁓ℰℐ

"Luke! Lexi! Don't leave me!" cried Roland.

"Crawl under the door!" Luke called, ecstatic to hear the familiar voice.

"I can't. I'm hurt," replied Roland. "Just open the door and let me out."

"But the door is locked," said Lexi, "and we have no key."

"It's only locked on the inside, to keep monsters *inside* the mountain," said Roland.

Sure enough, Luke easily pulled the door open. Roland stumbled toward them out of the darkness, squinting in the blinding daylight. All three found themselves on a small ledge above a steep, grassy slope.

"You're alive!" Lexi cried, impulsively hugging Roland.

"*You're* completely covered in dirt!" Roland smiled.

"So you forgot to warn us about that big fish back there . . ." Luke said drolly.

"Would you have been willing to navigate the Catacombs of Atsash if I had?" asked Roland.

"Of course not!" Luke answered.

"See! That's why I couldn't tell you!" Roland said. "We would have certainly been caught if we had taken the overland route. We were better off taking our chances with the lake monster."

"I am so glad you are all right!" Lexi interrupted, hugging Roland again. "I thought you were dead!"

"Well," Luke mused, "since it was your idea and you were the one who almost got eaten, I suppose all's well that ends well. By the way, where are we?"

The twins and dwarf turned their attention to the fantastic landscape. Behind them, the Saw Tooth Mountains stretched skyward into the clouds, while to the west they saw a long valley stretching north to south.

They had crossed under the entire mountain range. Before them lay a vast, verdant plain. Far in the distance, they could another range of mountains.

Hundreds of feet below, great herds of horses and unicorns galloped on the plain. In the sky there flew flocks of some unfamiliar bird. The surrounding slope consisted of nothing but grass and rocky outcroppings for miles and miles. White flowers dotted the green expanse like snow.

Despite their amazement, the twins found the scene oddly familiar. Lexi felt like she was trying to remember a dream—where had she seen this sight before?

Then, moving toward them along a narrow trail, they saw a bright-eyed girl near their own age. She carried a basket in one arm and reminded Lexi of Alysia's faeries. Like the Wrangland faeries, she walked barefoot, but wore two neat braids, a pretty blue frock and a white apron.

"Hello, Miss!" cried Roland.

"You must be the prince and princess," the girl addressed Luke and Lexi, turning to Roland, she continued, "and you must be their guide and companion."

"How did you know who we were?" Luke asked, baffled.

"My mistress sends aloe for your wounds," said the girl, kneeling before Roland. She began treating the deep scratches on his legs.

She looked up at the twins and continued, "My mistress has been expecting you. She sends a loaf and some milk to break your long fast."

The girl pulled out some sweet-smelling bread and a jar of fresh milk and passed them to the weary travelers.

"Who is your mistress?" asked Lexi, still not sure if it was safe to eat the girl's food.

"Why, Miriam, of course!" replied the girl with the braids. "She has been expecting you."

When the travelers were refreshed, the party followed their new companion along the narrow path, until they came to another opening in the face of the mountain. They saw another ledge and two seated figures.

Lexi instantly recognized the ancient, white haired man, who napped in a plush chair. A tiny old woman sat beside Timothy, with her dark hair pulled back in a bun. The old man snored contentedly, but the woman peered at the travelers.

"You must be Princess Lexi and Prince Luke," the old woman said.

"My Lady." Roland took a knee, despite his injuries.

"How good to see you again, Roland, my boy," said Miriam. "I am sorry to hear about Megan getting captured. You will be reunited soon, though."

"How does she know that?" Lexi whispered to her brother.

"I know many things," Miriam addressed the princess. "The heavens reveal themselves to those with open eyes and pure motives."

"I don't understand," said Lexi.

"You will, child," Miriam assured her, before turning to Luke. "So here stands the future king of Nèra Toli. Stand up straight. Keep your hands out of your pockets."

"Yes, ma'am," Luke saluted instinctively.

"It is a good thing you have a few years yet to prepare for the throne," Miriam sighed. "There is still much to learn."

"What do you mean?" asked Luke. "My father is dead. That makes me the rightful king right now. That is why we have come to you and Timothy for help."

"All in good time, my boy," the mysterious woman smiled.

Just then, their old tutor awoke with a snort. Timothy fumbled for his spectacles and greeted the travelers.

"Luke! Lexi! How are my two favorite students?" he said, smiling.

"We're your *only* students!" said Lexi, grinning. The twins gave their tutor a hug. Lexi buried her face in the old man's shoulder the way she had since she had been a little girl.

He still smelled of pipe tobacco: It was a sweet, familiar smell. His whiskers tickled her cheek and she pulled away to look at the old man again.

"Timothy, everything has been simply horrid since you left!" Lexi cried.

"Have a seat," Timothy laughed merrily like Old Man Winter. "Have a cup of tea and tell me about your journey.

"Ah, Roland, at last!" he continued, "How nice to meet you! Miriam has been telling me all about you."

The three travelers sat down in soft chairs that they had not noticed before. Miriam produced a tea service and soon everyone was enjoying tea and crumpets as if it were any other afternoon back at the castle.

Luke, for one, was bursting at the seams to tell Timothy about all their adventures.

"Count Damien has made everyone think that *we* killed Father!" he exclaimed. "Nana sent us away before they could arrest us, but they have been chasing us ever since."

Lexi continued, "We escaped into the Wranglands with John Boy and then Megan led us through the forest. Then we met Wolfram. I thought he was going to eat us, but he turned out to be nice."

"Really?" intoned Timothy. "What would make you think that he would want to eat you?"

"He's a *wolf!*" Lexi replied. "Wolves *always* eat princes and princesses up, don't they?"

"Apparently not," Timothy said. "After all, you are still here. Besides, I understand that it is the wolves in wool suits that you should be wary of."

"Huh?" said Lexi.

"You know, the ones dressed like sheep," Timothy clarified. "Tell me more, children."

"We even got captured by Alysia, Queen of the Faeries, but we escaped," Luke explained. "We found out that Megan and Roland's parents got arrested by Count Damien's men because they helped us. Then we were ambushed and Megan was captured."

"That's where we all got separated," added Roland.

"They must have killed Wolfram, because they did not carry him back alive and we have seen no sign of him since," said Lexi.

"Then we went through the Catacombs of Atsash," Luke interrupted, "and nearly got eaten by a lake monster. We thought Roland drowned when our boat capsized—"

"But he caught up with us at the top of those horrible, endless stairs," Lexi added, "and here we are."

* * *

As they told Timothy their story, he stroked his long beard with one hand and held his pipe with the other. He knit his eyebrows and stared out into the distance, saying nothing.

"Well?" Lexi finally asked. "What do we do now?"

"I think . . ." Timothy spoke slowly, pausing for further reflection. "I think that the two of you will need some new shoes."

"What!" Luke cried. "We didn't come all this way just for new shoes!"

"If you plan on saving the kingdom from Count Damien's clutches, not to mention saving Megan and her parents, you will not want to be barefoot," the old man mused.

Lexi looked down at her feet. Her slippers were in shreds. How many miles had she walked in her delicate slippers? Her feet had little cuts in them and she had stubbed her big toe.

Timothy was right: If they were going to save the kingdom, they would need to recuperate from their journey. They were exhausted.

CHAPTER **XX**

THE LESSON OF THE UNICORN

ⴰⵔⵛⵢ ⵉⴰⵏⵏⵎⵛ ⵛⵡ ⵇ ⵡⴰⵔⴰ ⵡⴰⵇⵙ ⵙⵣⵏⵛ ⵡⵇ ⵢ

The next morning Luke woke up with a start. He was alone in a dark cave. For a moment, he wondered if he was back in the Catacombs of Atsash. Then he noticed dozens of candles burning in little shelves carved into the cave's limestone walls.

There were beautifully woven tapestries hanging elsewhere and ornately patterned rugs covering the floor. Luke pushed aside blankets and pillows and got to his feet. He saw two neatly made beds that must have belonged to Roland and Lexi. He hurried outside to find his companions.

The young prince ducked his head to pass under the low overhang at the mouth of the cave. He blinked his eyes in the blinding sunlight. On the ledge overlooking Unicorn Valley, Roland and Timothy were leisurely having tea and scones for breakfast.

"Where is Lexi?" Luke called.

"Good morning to you too!" replied Roland.

"All right, all right," harrumphed Luke. "Good morning, Roland. Good morning, Timothy. So where has Lexi gone?"

"She has gone with Miriam to pick Winter Sky, the blossom that blooms only at the Saw Tooth Summit," said Timothy.

"This is no time for hiking around and gathering bouquets," Luke said. "We have to get back to Nèra Toli and unseat Count Damien!"

"Patience, child," Timothy replied. "Yes, we are in haste, but there *is* such a thing as hurrying too much. If I climb all the way to my chamber but forget the key, I will have to go back and find it, climbing up all over again.

"I will be in an even greater hurry for all my efforts. So let us not to go so fast that we waste time. If you return to Nèra Toli without the key, you would be better off not going back at all."

"But why must Lexi and Miriam go off picking flowers, anyway?" Luke persisted.

"That is for them to know," Timothy said. "You, my boy, have much more to do than ponder their business."

Timothy gestured for Luke to sit down and eat. Luke needed no convincing. He laughed to think how he and his companions had come so far through the wilderness to be greeted with tea and savory pastries.

* * *

Within the hour, Timothy and Luke followed a narrow trail down the mountain. They walked on for what seemed like hours, until they finally reached the valley's floor. Great equine herds grazed on the wide plain before them.

The old man and young prince sat down on a rocky outcropping at the base of the mountain. As he relaxed, Luke looked at the horses grazing peacefully. He gasped. Not only were there herds of horses, but there were also unicorns.

Luke had seen a unicorn horn sword once before. It had been long like a rapier but harder than the finest steel.

"This is the sword used by my great-grandfather to fight raiders from the Sutherland," his father had said, showing him the opalescent weapon.

Since then, Luke had always longed for the day when he too would defend his country from the barbaric pirates that often attacked their coast.

After a long while, Timothy spoke. "Which is more noble, the unicorn or the horse?" he asked.

"The unicorn, of course!" answered Luke.

"Perhaps," said the old man, "or perhaps not. Watch the horses and that famed Monoceros, whose horn your people so treasure."

Luke glanced impatiently at the herds. He already knew that the unicorn was the rarest, most noble beast in all Nèra Toli. Bards sang of their beauty.

Horses, on the other hand, were plain and far from noble. Horses were beasts of burden. They were as boring as the wagons they pulled.

Just then, Luke noticed a young horse grazing alongside some nearby mares. A big, bay stallion came out of nowhere and drove the younger male away. The larger horse neighed at the fleeing interloper and returned to his females. After a while, the horses moved on.

"Tell me what just happened," Timothy said.

"Well, the stallions had a fight for the females and the small one ran away," Luke said.

"So why do you think the small horse ran away? Why did he not stand his ground?" Timothy asked.

"He probably ran away because he is just a coward. Horses are cowardly," the prince said dismissively. "That is why they have always been beasts of burden. We should watch the unicorns instead. They are far nobler."

"As you wish," Timothy sighed.

They did not have to wait for long before a small herd of ivory colored unicorns approached. The beautiful, horned beasts grazed just as the horses had. Before long, a nearby young male attracted the attention of the dominant stallion of the herd.

When the large unicorn tried to bully the young one, the latter fought back. Instead of biting and rearing, the unicorns attacked each other using their pearly horns.

Finally, blood was spilled. The young male turned to flee, but it was too late. The large male thrust his horn into his rival's belly.

The young unicorn fell, bleeding, in the grass in front of Luke and Timothy. The herd moved away from the dying unicorn, which looked mournfully at Luke before finally closing its eyes.

"Timothy, why did you bring me here?" Luke asked, angry and confused. "I thought unicorns were noble and brave."

"That young unicorn was noble and brave," answered Timothy, "but he was still smaller than his opponent. If he had no horn, he would have run away like a coward, but he would be alive tomorrow for his troubles."

"What are you saying?" Luke demanded. "My whole life, I have been taught that you have to prove yourself if someone challenges you to a fight. I don't want to be a coward like a common horse!"

"Listen to me, boy! I brought you here for a reason," said Timothy. "Two days hence, you will be back at your father's castle to wrestle the crown from Count Damien before he can defile your mother and usurp the throne.

"You must defeat him, but you are the small horse and he is the large stallion. He has chased you away. If you fight him on his terms, you will die as the smaller unicorn did when he challenged his larger rival.

"Your only strength is your swiftness. Once you draw your sword, he will have already defeated you."

"How can I defeat Count Damien if I can't fight him?" Luke retorted.

"You must expose his deceit before the people. They will support you and unseat him," said Timothy.

"It seems to me that if I refuse to fight Count Damien, he will kill me that much more easily," Luke objected.

"That is a possibility," said the old man. "But everyone would know that you are not a treacherous murderer as he claims. Your death would then be your victory."

"If my name is cleared after he slits my throat, how have I saved Nèra Toli?" asked Luke.

"After you accuse Count Damien, you must flee when he draws his sword," Timothy commanded. "Your victory will take care of itself. Your advantage is that you are still small and swift. His strength will be a burden as he pursues you. Every step will be harder on him than on you, so wear that villain out!"

"I wish I had your confidence that everything will work out," said Luke. "I suppose I really am a coward at heart."

The old man puffed at his pipe for a long while.

"A coward does nothing at all because the odds are not in his favor. A coward cares more about survival than honor," Timothy finally said.

"You are many things, Luke, but a coward is not one of them." Timothy gave the prince a hearty pat on the back. "Your only stumbling block, my boy, is this idea of bravery," he added.

"I want to be brave, even if it means dying," said Luke. "I want to punish Count Damien for killing my father. I want vengeance!"

"Yes, Count Damien deserves to be punished for his crimes," said Timothy. "But if you had to watch him suffer as much as he deserves to, I daresay you would beg the High King to show him mercy."

"What do you mean?" Luke furrowed his brows, puzzled.

"What Count Damien needs is a new heart. That is something only the High King can grant him," said Timothy. "Remember, it is better for you to die and walk with the High King, than to kill Count Damien and send him to judgment when he has learned nothing of love.

"Focus on *your* job. You must resist letting Count Damien seduce you into fighting him on his terms. *That* is bravery, my boy."

Luke murmured something under his breath. He wanted to be brave, but he always thought bravery meant fighting. He worried that when the time came, he would fail—running away, getting himself killed or getting blood on his hands.

They walked back to Miriam's cave in silence. Looking back at the plain, Luke saw the vultures gathered around the dead unicorn. He swallowed hard.

Chapter XXI
THE KING'S MAGIC

ꞩꞇꜱꝯ ꭗꞇꞇ ꭗꞅꞇꝯ ꞇꝯ

After breakfast, Miriam handed Lexi a pair of leather moccasins. "Put these on," the old woman instructed. "Let's get going."

"What do you mean?" asked Lexi, while she put on her earthy new shoes. They were elegant yet sturdy on the outside, and unbelievably soft on the inside.

"We are going on a little walk," Miriam said, slinging a bag over her shoulder. Despite Miriam's rustic attire, she had a stately manner about her.

"At the summit of this mountain," she continued, "there grows a flower called Winter Sky. They say that an elixir made of Winter Sky can cure any ailment, bringing people back from death's very door."

"So what?" Lexi said bitterly. "What good is this elixir to me? My father is already dead!"

"Walk with me, child," said Miriam, turning to face the mountain. "We will talk more in good time."

Lexi followed the old woman as she set off. Miriam moved quickly for being so old. With her walking stick in hand, Miriam led the way a narrow trail up the mountain. Lexi scrambled to keep up. Finally, panting and heart racing, the princess ventured, "Could we stop and rest for a little while."

"Not used to the elevation, eh?" the old woman laughed. Her black eyes twinkled with merriment while her bronze skin glowed.

Lexi suddenly realized that Miriam looked like an aged version of herself. The princess shivered, although it was not cold. The old woman and girl sat down next to a small spring.

* * *

"How much do you know about magic?" Miriam asked.

"Not much," Lexi shrugged. "I have heard that Timothy is one of the greatest magicians around, but I have never seen him utter so much as a single spell."

"Well, my dear, there are two types of magic in this world," began Miriam. "There is a magic—a mysterious *owk ays ehn ezh*—that is everywhere, in everything, woven into the fabric of universe by the one and only High King of Nèra Toli. Your tutor Timothy and I do only the King's Magic.

"Then there is another magic that is often summoned by those seeking knowledge, wealth and, most of all, power. It is seductive and selfish. Count Damien and his allies practice this other magic because it alone can give them what they seek—control of Nèra Toli.

"The King's Magic, on the other hand, cannot be used for our own prideful ends. The King's Magic is something that happens when doing the moral thing requires us to do the impossible."

"So why don't you and Timothy cast spells or make potions?" asked Lexi.

"The King's Magic has no need of accessories. We simply ask for what we need," replied Miriam.

"So why do I need to know about magic, anyway?" the princess asked, bewildered and annoyed.

"Let's walk a bit further," Miriam answered. "We have a long way to go to the top of the mountain." She motioned up toward where the mountain rose into the clouds.

At that, the old woman was on her feet again, trotting briskly up the trail. Although irritated at not getting a straight answer, Lexi shrugged and chased after her.

* * *

After another hour of climbing steep switchbacks, Miriam paused at another spring. She fished a small leather bag out of her satchel and offered the princess some dried fruit.

"No, thanks," Lexi said, turning up her nose at the unfamiliar dried dates and figs.

"Eat, child!" Miriam insisted. "How can you climb a mountain if you will not eat anything?"

"All right," the princess relented, extending her hand.

"You asked why you should know about magic. You have a special job ahead of you and you will need the King's Magic to do it," Miriam explained, chewing. "When you go back to Nêra Toli, your job will be to wake up your father."

"What are you talking about?" exclaimed Lexi, choking in surprise. "I thought we went over this! My father is dead! Count Damien poisoned him. That is why we fled here—we have been accused of assassinating him."

"Calm down, child," Miriam reassured the princess. "Your father is not dead. Yes, Count Damien poisoned him, but the poison did not kill him. No, Count Damien is not foolish enough to kill your father. Instead, the king sleeps soundly, but you will wake him up."

"How do you know he is still alive?" Lexi asked incredulously.

"I saw him in a dream," Miriam said, "a very vivid dream."

You have got to be joking! Lexi thought. Yet the old woman looked serious.

"It will take more than a dream to convince me that my father is still alive," Lexi said dismissively. "Why did the poison fail to kill him? Did your dream tell you that?"

"There is a powerful protection on the throne of Nêra Toli," Miriam replied. "Without supernatural protection, good kings have a way of meeting with unfortunate ends."

"What do you mean?" Lexi furrowed her brow.

"Good kings do not normally live long lives, in Nèra Toli or elsewhere," whispered Miriam, "so it is written that those who spill the blood of a righteous king will themselves die untimely deaths. Count Damien knows of this curse, so he dares not kill your father.

"Instead," Miriam went on, "he used a strong sleeping potion, so that your father would sleep his life away if left undisturbed. Yet His Highness is not dead. He only awaits a friendly voice to rouse him from his slumber."

"But someone would have noticed that Father was not really dead when they held his funeral," said Lexi. "They wouldn't just bury him alive, would they?"

"Your father slumbers so deeply that only the wisest healer would see that he still lives," said Miriam. "As for him being buried alive, did you not know that the deceased royalty of Nèra Toli rest in the crypt beneath the castle? Count Damien simply plans to descend to the crypt whenever the king needs another dose of medicine."

"So why am I the one to wake my father?" Lexi asked, still unconvinced.

"Someone has to wake him and your gifts make you well suited to the task," Miriam explained. "Besides, your brother will be too busy confronting Count Damien before the people of Nèra Toli."

"So you want me to give my father an elixir of Winter Sky to wake him up?" Lexi asked.

"Actually, Winter Sky itself does nothing," said Miriam. "The magic lies in believing that a cure will work."

"So I am supposed to administer Winter Sky and convince myself that it will heal him?" asked Lexi, confused again.

"You don't need Winter Sky to heal your father," Miriam said. "The spell cast on your father is easily broken. All you need is to trust the King's Magic."

Lexi raised her eyebrows. "I already told you I know absolutely nothing about magic," she said.

"What's to know?" Miriam reassured her. "You need only find your way down into the crypt and trust."

"But how do I *know* that it will work?" Lexi objected. "You are not even giving me any spell to say. You have just told me that the one elixir that could have cured him doesn't even do anything. And how can I be sure that Father is not really dead?"

"That is a good point," Miriam admitted. She paused for a moment before continuing. "You can never be sure *how* the magic will work—*that* is up to the High King. You can only *trust* that, whatever happens, the King's Magic is at work."

With that, Miriam stood up and dusted herself off. Miriam's answer left Lexi dissatisfied. The travelers continued up the mountain in silence. Miriam seemed to expect Lexi to say something, which made Lexi even more resistant to talking. The longer they walked, the harder it became for Lexi to break that silence.

* * *

162

Eventually, they reached the summit without either one of them having said anything in hours. Miriam enjoyed the silence, but Lexi wrestled with it.

A bitterly cold wind whistled about them. Miriam pulled a shawl out of her pack and wrapped it around herself. She pulled out another for Lexi.

"But if you think about it, the whole idea of magic is absurd!" Lexi finally blurted out, without even glancing at the spectacular view.

"I have seen Timothy do some pretty amazing things, but it makes a lot more sense that he just knows lots of fancy tricks to make it *seem* like magic is real."

"You are right, magic is impossible," Miriam said unexpectedly.

"But you said that magic was real," Lexi objected.

"It is real," Miriam explained. "The King's Magic is the impossible made real."

"But I don't understand," said Lexi.

"You don't have to," said Miriam. "You just have to trust. It will happen if it is supposed to happen."

"But how can I trust that impossible things will happen?" asked Lexi. "That makes no sense at all!"

"Impossible things happen every day," said Miriam. "It is only because the impossible happens so often that people are blind to it."

Lexi thought for a moment and began:

"I remember when Count Damien first came to the castle he brought a pet cat with him. One time I noticed that the cat had caught something, so Luke pried open its mouth. It was one of my mother's doves, but it was dead. Its neck was broken.

"We showed it to Timothy and he took it in his hands and rubbed back and forth a little bit. The bird stirred, sat up in his palm and flew away. Luke and I both saw him do it, but we still could not believe it."

"So you have seen the King's Magic at work with him," said Miriam.

Lexi glanced away and then looked up at Miriam again, saying, "Even though I saw him revive the dead bird, I still could not believe my eyes.

"I kept thinking that he must have had a live bird in his pocket and switched the birds somehow. I also wondered if the bird was really dead, or if it had only seemed like its neck had been broken."

"It is good that you do not automatically believe everything you see," said Miriam, "but you have to know when to say when. Anyone who knows Timothy can tell that he is honest, with no desire to deceive or impress anyone."

"I doubt Timothy cares one bit about impressing anyone," Lexi agreed, "and I have never seen him lie to anyone."

"You know Timothy well enough to know his motives," Miriam continued, "and he is no trickster. But it is easier to dismiss good men as liars than to believe the unbelievable."

* * *

Miriam looked to the west at the Unicorn Valley and east toward Nėra Toli. Even though Lexi was right there next to her, Lexi still seemed not to see the panoramic view.

"It's windy up here," Lexi said, shivering.

164

"It is tempting to dismiss what we don't understand," Miriam explained. "What separates the King's Magic from illusion or sorcery is that we do not cast spells or seek power."

"So, if you do not cast spells, what exactly do you do to make the King's Magic work?" Lexi said impatiently.

"Our job is to simply obey the King's command to love Him and each other. If we obey, He will help us to do whatever our job is, even if we don't understand how."

"It is just so hard to believe in something when you can't see how it works," said Lexi. "So what happens if I just *can't* bring myself to believe in the King's Magic?"

"Then your father will not wake up," said Miriam matter-of-factly.

"But he *has* to wake up!" Lexi insisted.

"Then believe me when I tell you that he *will* wake up," said Miriam. "If I told you that all you had to do was administer an elixir of Winter Sky and he would wake up, you would have an easy enough time believing me."

"Of course I would," Lexi said. "Everyone knows that Winter Sky has special healing properties."

"What matters is that, with or without elixirs, all healing comes from the Maker of this incomprehensible magic that holds the universe together, from Aushey Himself."

"Who?" asked Lexi.

"The High King, of course," said Miriam. "That is why it is called the King's Magic, after all."

"But I thought that the High King was dead," the princess objected, "if he ever existed at all."

"Oh, yes. He was indeed dead," Miriam said. "But death itself broke when it broke His body."

"I don't get it," said Lexi.

"How could the Source of all life keep from being alive?" the old woman.

"If the High King lives, where is he now?" Lexi asked skeptically.

"Beyond the stars, beyond the very fabric of the sky," said the old woman, "awaiting the appointed time to return. Of course, He's also with us right now."

"Great! He's invisible! Very convenient!" said Lexi. "Far away in the heavens and right beside me all at the same time. So you want me to risk my life, trusting an invisible entity I've never met?"

"I know you haven't met Him, but I have," said Miriam. "Yes, trusting the High King is scary, but it's not like you have a lot of options."

"You have a point there," said Lexi.

"You can either keep running from Count Damien," Miriam continued, "or find some courage and save the kingdom."

Lexi looked out at the horizon, still unable to wrap her mind around Miriam's words. As her mind tried to stretch, she suddenly managed to take in the panorama before her. She gasped. The view took her breath away.

* * *

"What you should be thinking about is how to sneak down to the crypt without being seen," the old woman said after a long time.

"Oh, that part is easy!" laughed the princess. "Our father's castle is riddled with more secret passageways than *Latnemme* cheese."

"Indeed!" Miriam exclaimed. "I had no idea."

"I am surprised your dreams did not tell you about the castle's secrets," Lexi said mockingly.

"The High King uses dreams to tell me only what I need to know. Besides, if He provided all the details, there would be no surprises," Miriam chuckled.

"I know the way to the crypt once we are back inside the castle," Lexi said, serious again, "but how can we possibly get back inside the castle itself?"

"Why do you ask me, child? I thought this was your adventure," Miriam replied.

"We came here for help, not to be teased," Lexi said crossly. "It took us forever to get here and we have to be back there tomorrow. How in Nėra Toli are we supposed to get there in time to stop Mother from marrying Count Damien?"

"You are a perceptive little thing," Miriam smiled. "It sounds like you will need to pick up the pace on your return trip."

"We have been on the road all day for the better part of a week," Lexi objected. "And now our horse and Wolfram are gone, so we will have to walk the whole way. On top of that, I just *can't* go back inside the Catacombs of Atsash."

"Sounds hopeless," Miriam jested. "It's too bad about your father, though—just lying there waiting for someone to wake him up."

But Lexi didn't realize Miriam was being playful. She felt convicted. The fate of the king and of the whole kingdom depended on her. *There has to be a way!* she thought. All of a sudden, her eyes lit up.

"You know what I don't understand is how Timothy got here ahead of us," she said.

Miriam gave the princess a funny look, lifting an eyebrow. Before them to the west lay Unicorn Valley, stretching to the north and south as far as the eye could see. On the western horizon, they could see another range of mountains to the west beyond the valley.

To the east, Lexi could see the Meandering River's path all the way from the Saw Tooth Mountains to the sea. She was amazed at how far they had come in the past week.

"Timothy can barely walk without his staff," Lexi continued, "but he still got to your cave ahead of us. How did he do it?"

"That is an interesting question," Miriam said mysteriously. "Maybe you should ask him."

* * *

The next thing the old woman did was to pull out a little flute from her satchel and play a mournful, lilting melody. Lexi looked down.

The castle stood just north of the mouth of the river, but—squint as she might—the princess still could not see the familiar walls. From the mountaintop, Nera Toli looked serene and peaceful.

The princess had to remind herself that as peaceful as Nera Toli seemed, all was not right: she and her brother were wanted for murder—a murder that had never even happened. Their father was still alive!

A great pegasus landed in front of Miriam. She continued playing her flute until another winged horse joined the first. The old woman ended her song and put her flute away. The memory of Miriam's tune lingered in Lexi's ears.

"Well, what are you waiting for?" asked Miriam. "It is getting late. We have a long way to go." Miriam gracefully mounted one of the winged horses. "It is too late in the day for us to walk back down the mountain."

At first, Lexi clumsily struggled to get up on the back of her pegasus. Then the equine graciously knelt down so she could mount.

A minute later, the old woman and girl found themselves soaring down the mountain through cold, wet clouds and crisp alpine air. Riding a pegasus was much windier than Lexi had imagined.

Chapter XXII
TIMOTHY'S SHORTCUT

ꮞꮖꭹꭿꭼꭾꭶꮅꭺꭰꭲꭲ

Within a few minutes, the two mountain climbers were back at Miriam's cave, just in time to meet Timothy and the young prince. Luke stared in disbelief as Miriam and Lexi dismounted from their winged steeds in the chilly afternoon air.

The four companions soon sat in a comfortable chamber, enjoying a hearty stew and fresh bread. Lexi kept glancing out the window overlooking the valley. The view seemed oddly familiar.

"So we had a nice little walk today," said Miriam with her gift for understatement.

"How marvelous," Timothy replied, contentedly puffing his pipe. He paused to cough deeply.

"You really should quit," Luke said authoritatively.

"Oh poppycock!" the wizard objected. "I have been smoking this pipe since before your ancestors even arrived in Nèra Toli from the Northlands and I still have quite a bit of kick in me."

"Well, you are not as spry as you used to be," said Lexi. "In fact, I was just wondering how you arrived here ahead of us when you are in such terrible shape. After all, you did not really have that much of a head start."

At that, Timothy gave a hearty laugh. "I was wondering when you would start asking questions," he said, his eyes twinkling.

"So?" asked Luke. "How *did* you beat us here? We got to ride, after all, and you only walked."

"I cheated," Timothy said, "or rather, I took a shorter route while you took the long way."

"But what do you mean?" asked Lexi. "We took the shortcut through the Catacombs of Atsash, but you were still ahead of us."

"I am an old man," Timothy began. "I do not have the strength to climb miles of stairs in the dark. No, I took an even better shortcut."

"If I may say so, that is a particularly fine view," Roland motioned to the window. He had been so quiet that the twins had forgotten he was there at all.

When Luke and Lexi turned to the window overlooking Unicorn Valley, they each suddenly got goose bumps. The view was the same as the image in the enchanted picture hanging in Timothy's tower. There was one large window on the western wall of the cave, and it looked just like Timothy's painting.

"Wow! A magic painting, just like in your tower!" Luke exclaimed. He could even see the horses and unicorns grazing, and the pegasus flying gracefully, just as in the magic picture back in the castle.

"It isn't a picture, you goon!" Lexi said. "It's a window. It just has the same view as the magic picture. Obviously, the magic painting is based on the view from this window."

"Why not take a look at the window from outside?" suggested Timothy, holding his teacup in both hands.

The twins left the cozy cave to examine the window from the outside. There was nothing remarkable about it. Looking through it, they saw Timothy and Roland.

Both Luke and Lexi felt foolish for going outside just to look back through the window at their companions. As they were about to go back inside, Luke noticed something.

"I thought there was only one window," he said, pointing. He pointed to another window to the left of the window to the cave. The prince and princess walked over to the other window and looked through it.

Like the first window, it had no glass pane. Instead of looking into a cave, the twins found themselves peering past a cluttered desk into a circular stone room.

"It's Timothy's tower!" cried Luke.

"That makes no sense," Lexi objected. Why should there be a picture of the inside of Timothy's tower hanging outside like this? Such a painting would surely get ruined by the elements. No one hung paintings outdoors. What had Miriam been thinking?

"Don't you understand?" exclaimed Luke. "This is a window into Timothy's tower!"

"But . . ." Lexi said, perplexed.

"It is not a window," Timothy explained, appearing behind the twins. "Rather, it is a portal."

"A real portal?" asked Luke. "How do you keep it from closing in on itself?"

"Not to get too technical, but the window panes have special properties," said Timothy. "It's open to discussion whether it's Phantom or Casimir energy that keeps such portals open. At any rate, the window panes exert an outward force that counteracts the portal's tendency to close in on itself."

"I'm sorry I asked," Luke muttered. "It's all *Kerg* to me."

"You mean *Keerg*," Lexi said patronizingly. Her brother's knowledge of *Keerg* and *Eip* was terrible for a future king. Languages were one of her strengths. Luke preferred falconry and swordplay to pouring over books.

"So this is how you got here so fast!" Luke cried. "I knew you must have had something up your sleeve!"

The old man smiled sheepishly, glad to be caught.

"Wait a minute!" Lexi interrupted. "Do you mean that I could just step through this window right now and be back at the castle?"

"I would not advise it," Timothy warned. "You do not have any supplies packed and you would be better off getting a good night's rest first."

* * *

When Lexi brushed her dark hair before bed, she almost forgot that she was on an adventure at all. She was so comfortable since arriving at Miriam's caves that she felt as if she were home again in her own room.

It would be a big change going back to her life as a sheltered princess. As exhausting as their journey had been, she would miss the freedom of the open road and the excitement of not knowing what each new day would hold.

The princess remembered with a shudder that they not home free yet: They still had to save the kingdom. Nothing was certain until this was all over. She tried to remember all the things Timothy and Miriam had said after dinner.

The plan was for Luke to confront Count Damien, while Lexi revived the king. Lexi thought about Megan, Megan's parents, John Boy and Nana. All of them sat in the castle's dungeon awaiting execution, all thanks to Luke and her.

Everyone who helped them wound up in trouble, the princess thought gloomily. Timothy had insisted that they wait to free the captives until after deposing Count Damien, but Lexi had her doubts.

What if they failed? Then their friends would have no chance at all. Finally, the princess laid down her worried head. She had fitful dreams all night.

The next thing Lexi knew, Miriam was shaking her.

"It is time to get ready," the old woman announced.

Lexi felt numb as she dressed herself and laced her new moccasins. Her hands felt swollen and clumsy; she wondered absently whether she was in shock. She could not taste her breakfast.

Before she knew it, they were in front of Miriam's cave, ready to pass through Timothy's portal. Timothy and Miriam gave the twins a few final words of advice.

Lexi saw their lips moving, and she could hear sounds, but she could not understand anything they said. Her brain had no room for words. She kept thinking that she would never see them again, that she and Luke would be dead within a day.

No! Lexi corrected her thinking. *My father is alive, and the High King will protect us.*

Somewhere deep down, she knew that focusing on the truth and on their goal was the difference between life and death.

"Good luck," Roland said, squeezing Lexi's hand.

She bent down to be level with the dwarf. He was not just a dwarf anymore. He was a human being. He was her friend. Of course, he had always been a human being. She was the one who had been blinded by tradition.

"Thank you for all your help. I know we will win back the kingdom," Lexi said, hoping to convince herself.

"I know *you* will win back the kingdom," replied Roland.

"I thought you were coming with us," Lexi said, caught off guard.

"I'll be along shortly," said Roland. "You have your tasks, I have mine."

Almost before Lexi knew what was happening, Luke took her by the hand. Together, they stepped through the painting that hung on the side of Miriam's mountain.

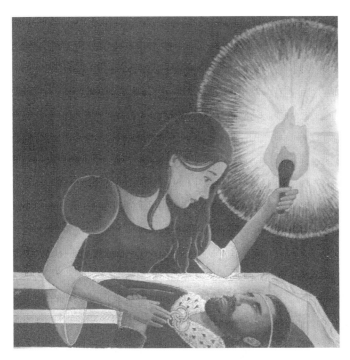

Chapter XXIII
THE SLEEP OF DEATH

ᏰᏃᏋᎴᏋᎴᏋᏋᎴᎴᏋᎴᏋᏃᏋᏋᏋ

Timothy's tower was windier, damper and darker than the twins remembered it. There was no crackling fire to give it a comfortable, homey feel.

The tower had a gray, predawn quality to it. Despite the darkness, they could see that it had been completely ransacked.

"How did this room get so messy?" asked Lexi, gingerly avoiding a large, overturned tome.

"It looks like Count Damien's men were searching for Timothy," said Luke, examining the destruction.

"But I thought Count Damien dismissed him even before we fled," Lexi objected.

"You would find it odd, would you not, if you fired someone and he just disappeared into thin air?" said Luke.

"He must have thought that Timothy never left in the first place!" Lexi gasped.

"Let's go," said Luke. "If we stick around here much longer, we're sure to be caught and hung before long."

The twins crept down the stairs. At the foot of the spiral staircase, a burly guard snored peacefully. Slipping past him was almost too easy. Even still, when the guard moved in his sleep, Lexi nearly jumped out of her skin.

* * *

Within a few minutes, Luke and Lexi were safe inside their secret passageway. Luke's task was to accuse Count Damien before the people, while Lexi was to revive their father.

The twins parted ways at the fork in the tunnel. Lexi descended the stairs to the crypt, while Luke headed to the balcony.

"Good luck, Luke!" cried Lexi.

"Give Father my regards, if Count Damien does me in," said Luke.

"Don't talk like that!" Lexi scolded. "Everything is going to be fine. Just trust in the King's Magic."

"That's easy for you to say," said Luke. "No one is going to lop your head off if the Magic doesn't work."

Luke drew his finger across his throat for emphasis.

"We can trade jobs if you want to," said Lexi, "but you don't seem to be falling all over yourself to go down to the crypt."

"Well, we might both wind up there before the day is through," Luke said ominously. "What does it matter, anyway? At least we will go down with honor."

At that, the twins parted ways. Luke continued toward the royal balcony while Lexi descended the stairs toward the crypt. Soon, their two torches were out of sight from one another.

* * *

Lexi opened the door to the crypt. She felt a cold draft and her torch flickered. She had explored the castle's secret passageways, but had never ventured down into the crypt. People said it was haunted by the ghosts of tormented kings.

There was a walkway going down the middle of the room, with crystal caskets on either side. She could see the remains of the deceased through the caskets.

She saw one particularly ornate, bejeweled casket and her eyes lingered on it. Inside, was a wizened, wasted body in beautiful robes.

The princess wondered which ancestor she was looking at and suddenly felt sick. She vomited on the floor and felt embarrassed, even though there was no one around. Lexi continued onward.

When she was halfway through the long room, Lexi started trembling. How would she recognize her father's casket? How could she wake him up if she could not even find him? Lexi felt panicky and thought about turning back. Just then, something caught her eye.

In the crystal casket at the far end of the room lay the bulky form of a man. She rushed over. Of course! Her father had only been there a week, so his body had not had time to decompose. The king's features were still handsome and lifelike. *It's as if he is only sleeping*, Lexi thought.

She reminded herself that he *was* merely sleeping. *Maybe it just takes a while for corpses to look like corpses,* Lexi found herself thinking. Just because he looked good did not mean he was alive. The princess scolded herself for thinking like that. Did she want the King's Magic to work or not?

She bit her lip and pried up the lid of the casket. It was a lot heavier than it looked—she could barely move it. Then, just when she got the lid moving, it slipped and crashed to the floor, shattering. The king flinched. Lexi took heart and started shaking him.

"Papa, Papa!" she shouted. "Wake up, Papa!"

He did not stir. The princess wondered if she had only imagined that he flinched.

"Please wake up, Papa!" she cried. "Wake up! Wake up!"

Lexi heard her own shrieks echoing against the stone walls. The echoes sounded hysterical, even frightening.

"They said you would wake up! You have to wake up, Papa!" she cried. Finally, she threw herself across her father's body, sobbing. With her last ounce of strength, she commanded, "By the King's Magic, wake up!"

He stirred. Not a lot, but he definitely stirred. Lexi grabbed her father's cold hand and started rubbing it. She repeated over and over, "Wake up! Wake up! Wake up!"

Just then, the king's hand jerked. He pulled it up to his mouth and issued a deep, rumbling cough. He slowly sat up, looked at Lexi and said, "What's wrong, my raggle-taggle princess?"

Lexi burst into tears. He was alive! He was really alive! The king patted his daughter's dark hair as she sobbed. He slowly examined their surroundings. "What are we doing down in the crypt?" he said.

"You were dead. Count Damien killed you," Lexi began, "but Miriam told us you were still alive. I was afraid to get my hopes up, but she said you only needed someone to wake you up, and it was true— you are alive!"

The princess looked at her hands and realized that she was shaking. Now that they were safe, she was a nervous wreck.

"What do you mean I was dead?" asked the king.

"Count Damien gave you some sort of sleeping potion," Lexi explained, "but made it look like Luke and I murdered you."

"Indeed!" the king said, still dazed. "Where is Luke now?"

"He has gone to accuse Count Damien before the people," said Lexi.

The king suddenly became more lucid. "But until the people see me alive, they will still think me dead," the king exclaimed. "They will think Luke is lying!"

For a moment, Lexi looked puzzled as she tried to wrap her mind around her father's words.

"Count Damien will have Luke arrested and killed!" the king continued, bolting upright. "We must get to Luke immediately!"

"Agreed!" cried Lexi. "Let's go!"

The king crawled out of his crystal casket with some effort. It pained Lexi to think that a day would come when he would again rest in the crypt. She shook the thought out of her head.

A moment later, they were on their way. They returned the way Lexi had come, climbing the narrow stone stair to where she had parted from her brother.

They hung the torch on the wall and opened the small wooden door. Lexi ducked slightly and stepped through. The king stooped to follow her.

Before them hung a heavy tapestry. They moved to the edge, peeked first and then stepped out into the passageway.

Chapter XXIV
TRIAL BY COMBAT

ဠၗၐႚၐၕႜၐၒၚႜၒၔ႙ၐၑႚ

Luke hung up his torch, opened the little wooden door and ducked to pass through it. Before him hung the heavy tapestry that covered the entrance to the secret tunnel.

He moved to the edge of the wall hanging and stepped out into the light. The hallway was empty. Luke walked toward the balcony, where he knew he had to accuse Count Damien of his crimes.

As Luke walked down the passageway, he recalled the last time he had been there. It had been only a week before, but it seemed like a lifetime. He had been so carefree, little suspecting the treason Count Damien and Professor Albert planned.

Only now that his life was on the line did Luke feel as somber as a future king should. Only a week ago, his father had spoken to his people. Now the king rested in the bowels of the castle.

Luke stepped into the comfortable salon and, before he could second-guess himself, out onto the balcony. In the courtyard below, people were already setting everything up for the wedding.

He wondered if he should wait for the wedding before confronting Count Damien. His heart pounded in his chest, ready to explode. There was no way he could wait that long.

He grabbed the herald's trumpet that hung on the wall, took a deep breath and blew as hard as he could. An unexpectedly majestic sound erupted from the trumpet. Everyone looked up at the prince.

"Greetings, people of Nėra Toli!" Luke began. "As you know, my father was poisoned seven days ago."

Many in the courtyard started booing and shaking their fists at the prince. Luke narrowly dodged an apple someone hurled at him.

"Wait! It wasn't me! It was Count Damien!" Luke shouted. "Only he dared not kill my father, but gave him a sleeping potion instead."

While the people murmured below, the count himself emerged into the courtyard from the shadows. Count Damien was richly dressed for his wedding and crowning. He wore white, gold and diamonds from head to toe.

"Seize that lying villain!" Count Damien ordered, drawing his sword and pointing at the prince.

Half a dozen guards leaped toward the balcony. Luke remembered his old teacher's admonition not to fight and resigned himself to the knowledge that he would probably be dead within the hour. The prince picked up his heels and fled.

Here I am, a fool about to die a fool's death, he thought. Luke ran with every ounce of strength he had. Before long, he lost Count Damien's metal clad henchmen. He paused for a breath in the hallway and wondered what he should do next.

Just then, Count Damien himself appeared at the other end of the corridor. He strode confidently and arrogantly toward the prince, his sword in hand.

* * *

The king and princess stepped out into the hallway. They headed toward the royal balcony to find Luke.

"There they are! Get them!" someone shouted.

King Simon and Lexi ran to the salon and out onto the balcony, away from their pursuers. The crowd below them began to murmur.

Lexi and King Simon looked down and saw that every eye was upon them. The king raised his right arm in greeting and the crowd went wild.

"I still live," the king announced. "Count Damien dared not call down the Assassin's Curse upon himself. My daughter has awakened me and here I am."

The cheering crowd drowned out King Simon's words. *Everything is going to be all right,*

Lexi thought to herself. Just then, something struck her across the back of her head. Everything went black.

* * *

Count Damien's henchmen seized the princess and king and dragged them off. Albert the Clever stepped out onto the balcony.

"The king is *dead!*" he shouted, "First, these assassins killed him and now they seek to replace him with a conjured imposter. These sorcerers will die a fitting death—at the stake!"

The crowd was obviously confused now and strangely quiet. Most of them murmured in a low voice.

"The only imposter is Count Damien!" shouted a toothless old man. "The only sorcerer I see is *you!*" He pointed a gnarled finger accusingly at Albert.

Before the crowd could react to the old codger's words, arrows rained downed upon him. The elderly man fell down dead. A little boy ran up to him and threw himself on the old man's body.

"Grandpa! Grandpa!" the little boy cried. "Please get up, Grandpa!"

The young boy looked up and saw scores of armed men on the castle walls, bows drawn. More of Count Damien's men stepped forward out of the shadows, their swords drawn.

The crowd drew closer together, away from the soldiers. Even though they still outnumbered Count Damien's men, they were unarmed commoners. If any of them drew attention to themselves, they faced the old man's fate.

"As I was saying," Albert continued, "we will shortly dispose of those treasonous villains and their imposter king. "Count Damien is currently apprehending that knave of a prince, Luke, for the bonfire." Albert paused, smirked wickedly and went on. "Since Queen Tabitha is so fond of tapestries, I would also like to present her with a *hanging* as her wedding present."

The smirking young professor motioned with a flourish. Count Damien's toadies tied the king and princess to stakes, with kindling at their feet. They were going to be burned alive! Meanwhile, formidable men led Megan, her parents, John Boy and Nana to the gallows. Megan bit her captor and was socked in the ear for her trouble.

Everyone who had helped them was now doomed to die. *No good deed goes unpunished,* Lexi thought bitterly. *Where is this High King of Miriam's, Who so loves justice?*

Standing next to Professor Albert, Queen Tabitha looked on with glassy eyes, as if in a trance. *Wake up, Mother! Wake up!* Lexi screamed silently.

* * *

Count Damien looked invincible as he strode toward Luke. Rather, he looked as if he thought himself invincible, Luke observed. Count Damien smirked as he strutted forward, clad in gaudy white and gold wedding attire.

I'm not dead yet! Luke thought, recognizing his opponent's hubris. *He celebrates too soon.*

At that moment, Luke wanted nothing more than to drive his sword into Count Damien's belly.

187

The prince was shocked to find himself thinking such thoughts and shook his head as if to banish them.

Meanwhile, the count steadily approached. Luke resolved not to draw his sword, just as Timothy had warned him. Even though Timothy's commitment to non-violence did not make much sense to Luke, the prince trusted his old tutor.

A moment later, Luke darted away, with no idea where he was going.

Maybe I can get back through Timothy's painting to safety, he thought. Instead, Luke found himself running toward the east tower.

The last time he had been in the east tower had been that final morning before his fateful adventure had started. Luke wished in vain that he could escape to the safety of the past.

He could hear Count Damien's heavy breathing at his heels. When he reached the stairs up the east tower, he sprinted with all his might. He used to race his sister up those stairs in happier times and she would always beat him.

Luke wished that Lexi could have been there to see him set a new stair climbing record. Count Damien's breathing sounded heavier than ever, but more distant. When Luke reached the top of the tower, he closed the trapdoor to the stairs. He was safe!

Then, looking around the small room, he realized he was now trapped. It was only a matter of time until Count Damien hacked open the door.

Maybe I can hide, he thought, eyeing the few pieces of furniture. He glanced at the window and wished he could fly to safety. Just then, he heard Count Damien pound on the door at his feet.

Luke hurried to the window. *Of course,* he thought, *the roof!* Luke carefully pulled himself up onto the roof of the tower. He moved away from the window and frantically hoped that Count Damien would give up and go away.

The prince glanced longingly down at his sword, which was still in its sheath. He reminded himself not to draw his sword to fight, no matter what.

Not fighting went against every instinct he had, but he trusted Timothy and Miriam. He wanted to trust in the King's Magic in which they had so much confidence. Just then, Luke heard the door to the tower give with one last whack of Count Damien's broadsword.

The count was all the more furious for his exertion. If Luke could have seen him, he would have lost heart. Count Damien's skin was flushed with murderous rage. Even the veins in his neck were swollen. His red skin contrasted sharply with his elegant white robes.

"Where are you?" demanded Count Damien. "You miserable excuse for a prince! You are a *nothing*—too cowardly to fight like a man!" The count stormed around the room until he was sure that Luke was not there.

"What did you do, fly away?" the count shouted, leaning out the window. "What kind of bird are you, anyway? Don't you know that chickens can't fly!"

Luke tried to stay perfectly still when he heard the count. As if to spite him, his leg twitched and knocked a loose shingle down. Luke held his breath, but the shingle landed square on Count Damien's head. It did not hit hard enough to hurt him, but it certainly got his attention.

The count looked up and saw the prince. With renewed rage, he heaved himself up onto the roof. Luke backed up until the roof sloped down again behind him.

There was nowhere to go. Luke looked down at the filthy moat and wondered what it would feel like to hit the water from so high up.

"This is the part where you draw your sword," Count Damien laughed smugly. "Ah, I see—you are still too dignified to fight."

"I have the King's Magic on my side!" Luke shouted, trying to convince himself.

"Well, I have strength, steel and brains on mine!" retorted the count. "Why in Nėra Toli *did* you bother coming back to die?"

"I could not let you keep my father half-alive, half-dead down in the crypt forever," Luke said, darting out of the path of Count Damien's sword.

"So you plan on keeping him company, do you?" Count Damien smirked.

"You saw with your own eyes," said Luke. "My sister woke him up." He felt stronger at the thought that the king still lived. "If you kill me today, you will call the Assassin's Curse down upon yourself."

"The Assassin's Curse only protects kings, not princes. You, my boy, will never be king," Count Damien said coldly before lunging at Luke. He

190

delivered a glancing blow to the prince's arm, drawing first blood. Luke scrambled up the conical roof and clung to the flagpole. The banner above him fluttered in the wind.

It took every ounce of Luke's strength to resist drawing his sword. *Why did I bring this foul thing if not to fight?* he wondered bitterly.

He had made it this far following Timothy and Miriam's advice. Still, he wondered if he was just a fool.

"Do you want to know why you will never be king?" Count Damien demanded. "It is because you are an idealist and a coward—an unfortunate combination!"

As the count swung his sword, Luke dodged out of the path of the steel blade. The sword rung as it hit the flagpole.

"You believe in silly faery tales and magic," the count sneered. "In Nėra Toli, like everywhere else, the winner is the one with the better sword.

"Winners entertain no silly ideas about magical protection. If you are to be king, you have to want it more than anything else in the world."

"Well, I *don't* want the crown enough to kill for it—not even scum like you!" Luke retorted. Count Damien swung at the prince again. Once more, the prince escaped and the pole absorbed the blow.

At the latest impact, the narrow pole made a cracking sound and slowly tipped sideways. Luke steadied himself on the steep rooftop, but Count Damien again struck the pole. Luke tried to regain his balance, but the edge of the roof rushed toward him.

As he fell, time seemed to slow down. Luke miraculously managed to draw his sword and plunge it through the roof of the tower. He held on with all his might, as his body slammed against the side of the stone tower.

It had only been a week since he had hung in nearly the same place. This time there was no one to offer him a helping hand. He would live or die by his own strength today.

Count Damien confidently approached the dangling prince. "You may not want the crown enough to kill for it, but *I* do. You were born into the lap of luxury, but I had to work to get ahead. I have learned that if you want something in life, you have to go and take it."

The count approached the spot where Luke's sword was lodged in the roof. With one foot, Count Damien kicked the prince's hands, which clung to the hilt of the sword. Just then, in a split second, another loose shingle gave way and the towering villain's foot slipped out from under him.

It was the same loose spot that had betrayed Luke's presence only a few minutes before, the same spot that nearly sent Luke plunging to his death a week earlier.

The count waved his arms wildly, trying to steady himself. He screamed as he fell headlong over the edge of the rooftop. A few seconds later, there was a distant splash as Count Damien landed in the moat below.

Luke strained to pull himself back up onto the roof, his injured knuckles aching. His arms burned. He was so exhausted from hanging there that even the idea of falling sounded preferable to hanging on indefinitely.

He thought of the King's Magic and how it had seen him through his ordeal with Count Damien. He scolded himself for even thinking of giving up. Luke imagined the count's drowned body in the moat below and felt grateful to still be alive.

He and his sister had endured so many trials over the past seven days—Queen Alysia's seductive promise of safety, the Caverns of Atsash, the lesson of the unicorn. Now all he had to do was pull himself up and it would be over.

Luke summoned all his strength and somehow willed himself upward. He climbed back to the summit of the east tower and stood up. Just then, Luke noticed some fabric at the edge of the roof. He recognized the royal emblem. The prince picked up the fallen flagpole, faced the courtyard and waved.

Chapter XXV
TRIAL BY FIRE

As Count Damien's henchmen tied her to the stake, Lexi looked at her father. *How ironic,* she thought bitterly, *I woke him from a deathlike, perpetual slumber only to bring about his real death.* Lexi winced as the rope pinched her wrists.

"Daddy!" Lexi called. "Please forgive me for getting you into this mess!"

"I would rather die with you now than hover between life and death forever," said the king.

"I would rather not die at all, if you asked me," came a voice from the gallows.

194

"John Boy!" Lexi exclaimed.

"Look what comes of running off without me!" said John Boy. "Just because I twisted my ankle, you didn't have to leave me behind."

"Quiet there!" an armed guard hit John Boy with the hilt of his sword. Lexi recognized Zared, the attacker from the 'Beaten Path Roadhouse' whose life she had spared.

"I see you didn't die of thirst!" Lexi called out to him.

"Thank you for your kindness, Princess," Zared smiled. "It's a good thing you gave me a glass cup instead of pewter. Otherwise, I never could have cut my bonds."

"I should have let them kill you!" cried Lexi.

"Never regret showing someone mercy!" said King Simon. "I would rather there be blood on his hands than on yours."

"Father, it feels like everyone's blood is on my hands!" cried Lexi. She looked at Megan and her diminutive parents, John Boy, and good old Nana.

"Do not think like that," said the king. "You and your brother did the best you could. We all have to meet the High King someday. Today is as good a day as any."

Lexi looked away from her father. She had always assumed she would live to old age. Never in her worst nightmares had she considered the possibility of being burned alive. She had barely even begun to live and already it was time to die.

Worst of all, everyone who had helped her— John Boy, Nana, Megan and her parents—now faced death too. Lexi noticed that Goodman and Goodwife

Short's nooses hung lower than the rest. She chuckled unexpectedly.

Speaking of dwarves, Lexi suddenly wondered where Roland was. *Perhaps he fled to the Dwarf Kingdom,* she thought, *leaving us all to die.* Roland had always thought it was a bad idea to come back and unseat Count Damien. *No!* Lexi corrected her thoughts, *Roland would never leave us.*

After their long journey together, Lexi still had mixed feelings about Roland. She always felt so comfortable when she was with him, but he was still a dwarf, born of dwarf parents.

She knew what it would mean if they ever wed: According to custom, marrying someone who was dwarf-born meant she would forfeit both her royal title and lands.

For a split second, Lexi wished Count Damien's men would just light the fire and finish her off. At least it would rescue her from choosing between Roland and the world.

"People of Nèra Toli," announced Albert, "your future king is currently disposing of the treacherous, albeit persistent, Prince Luke. Now we will deliver justice to King Simon's other assassins."

"King Simon lives!" a voice called from the crowd.

"Who said that?" shouted Albert. He motioned to the stakes where King Simon and the princess were bound. "This is not King Simon. King Simon is dead! This is nothing but an imposter!"

Another voice called out, "King Simon lives!"

"Hang the accomplices!" Albert ordered. "Burn the princess and the imposter!" A moment later, the trapdoors beneath the gallows opened and the nooses tightened.

It was only when she actually saw the fire being kindled at her feet that Lexi realized just how much she wanted to live. The king and princess coughed from the thick smoke. There was a lot of smoke for such a small fire.

The next thing Lexi knew, there were firecrackers and sparklers going off. There was the sound of a thousand swarming bees all around. The princess felt the ropes that bound her loosen and fall away. As she felt herself being lifted up, she wondered if she had already died.

The fire had only just begun to lick her feet and now it was all over. She saw two winged beings at her side and wondered if they were the High King's messengers from the other side of eternity, come to take her home.

Then other figures emerged through the smoke. She saw her father and then Nana. There were Megan and her parents. All of them were held aloft by children with gossamer wings.

Queen Alysia's faeries had come to help them! Lexi saw John Boy, with four faeries frantically flapping their wings to keep his hefty frame in the air.

Other faeries had swarmed Count Damien's henchmen, sending them fleeing. Before long, the raucous quieted down and the smoke cleared. Lexi felt herself being set down on the balcony above the courtyard. Her feet buckled beneath her in pain, and she found herself caught up in Roland's short arms.

"I hope you'll forgive me," he said.

"What do you mean?" asked Lexi, confused.

"Your rescue was about thirty seconds later than planned," he said. "The burns on your feet will take a while to heal, but it could have been a lot worse!"

"You did this? You got help from Queen Alysia?" Lexi asked.

"I had to travel by pegasus to the Wranglands," said Roland, "and then Wolfram carried me the rest of the way. I've never seen him run so fast!"

A moment later, King Simon was deposited beside them. Straightening his royal robes, he turned to the dwarf and spoke, "Pardon me, sir, but I believe I owe you my gratitude."

"Anything for your daughter," said Roland. He made no attempt to hide his affection for Lexi.

"Well," the king cleared his throat, "Princess Lexi is already spoken for, you know. We've already made a match for her—an *acceptable* match."

"Look! Look!" Lexi exclaimed, pointing.

On the roof of the easternmost tower, a figure stood waving the royal banner. In a heartbeat, Lexi recognized her twin brother. In the courtyard below, people pointed toward the prince and started cheering.

* * *

"So he's dead then?" asked Megan.

"It is impossible to say for sure," said Luke. "Father's men have dredged the moat, but they found no body."

"Well, Count Damien is gone," said Lexi, "and that is enough for me!"

"And good riddance!" said Roland. "If he does come back, he can join Albert in the palace vault."

The four companions sipped tea and ate scones in the royal garden. Their lives were finally getting back to normal, but things were different now. They all felt older, much older.

Queen Tabitha was different too. Lexi had noticed that her mother was no longer cold and distant. Whatever spell she had been under had been broken. King Simon had changed too. He no longer treated Luke and Lexi like children, but with a newfound respect.

All the same, the twins were relieved to return to what remained of childhood. They could go back to schoolwork and learning royal manners, but they knew could never go back to being completely carefree.

"You know, I am glad we get to be kids for a little while longer," said Luke. "I was so eager to wrestle the crown from Count Damien, but it really is a relief not to be king just yet."

"It is a heavy burden to be king," said Megan. "It's a big sacrifice."

There was a long silence. All four knew without saying that Luke and Megan were in love. However, for Luke to remain heir to the throne, it would have to remain an unrequited love:

No one who was dwarf-born could join the royal line. Even though Megan was tall and beautiful, her parents were still dwarves, making her an unsuitable bride for the prince.

Luke didn't like to think of the young bride awaiting him. He was sure Princess Saskia was probably nice enough, but she was just a little kid. Although his marriage wouldn't take place for another seven years, Luke did not *ever* want to marry the unseen princess. He looked at Megan's bright eyes. *There has to be a way to make it work,* Luke thought.

Lexi and Roland faced the same quandary. Not only was Roland dwarf-born, but he was an actual dwarf. In order to someday marry him, she would have to give up her right of inheritance. If she married him, she too would become an outcast.

She looked at her brother, who would someday be the most powerful man in Nėra Toli. It would be truly ironic if she chose to become an outcast for love's sake, on the opposite end of the social spectrum from her royal birth.

I am the firstborn child of the king, she silently repeated her bitter mantra. *I should be heir to the throne. If only it hadn't been for Great-Great-Grandfather Ichabod...*

"I have a question," said Lexi, shutting out her jealous thoughts. "Why did Queen Alysia help us to defeat Count Damien?"

"Maybe she thinks father makes a better king than Count Damien," Luke suggested.

"Well, as much as she gives me the creeps," said Lexi, "we are in her debt."

"We do owe her our gratitude," Luke affirmed.

Megan looked uncomfortable. She cleared her throat and looked at her brother.

"We have lived in the Wranglands all our lives and have managed to avoid any major conflicts with Queen Alysia," said Roland. "The one thing I can say is that it's better not to owe her anything, because she will always remind you of your debt at the most inconvenient time."

"But make sure you stay on good terms with her and all the Fair Folk," said Megan. "As they say, 'Keep your friends close. Keep your enemies closer.'"

"Duly noted," Luke said.

"On a lighter note," said Lexi, "we can each look forward to sleeping in a real bed for a change."

Luke, Megan and Roland all laughed. It had been a long journey. Whatever mischief their enemies were planning, the companions were all safe for now.

* * *

The next day found the prince and princess back at their desks in Timothy's tower. Roland and Megan had returned home with their parents. Everything was back to normal.

As they conjugated irregular Dwarfish verbs, Lexi gazed dreamily at the scene behind Timothy's desk. She saw the vibrant landscape of Unicorn Valley, with its various grazing equines. Two winged horses chased each other in the vibrant blue sky.

Lexi smiled to think that she was not just looking at an enchanted painting, but at a real portal to adventure. She remembered Miriam's hospitality and looked at her brother. The twinkle in his eye told her that he had the same idea. The twins both raised their hands.

"Yes, children," said Timothy. "What is it? Are you finished already?"

"Can we go on a field trip?" the twins begged in unison. *"Pleeeease!"*

About the Author

From an early age, Francesca Giovanna Williams loved to explore both the natural world and that of books. An imaginative child, she longed for the extraordinary and sublime.

Francesca first discovered the fantasy novels of the Inklings in middle school. She was inspired to invent a land of her own and people to inhabit it. For years, she drew and redrew maps. Stories and images emerged. She eventually named her imaginary land "Nèra Toli."

Francesca and her husband have been married for fifteen years. They both grew up in Southern California and were childhood friends. They have wonderful children and a menagerie of critters. Francesca majored in Linguistics at the University of California, San Diego. She loves to write, draw, paint, sew, quilt, knit, study languages and go bicycling in her rare idle moments.

As far back as she can remember, Francesca wrestled with life's big questions. Fascinated and challenged by the Bible, she struggled with the idea of the existence of God and of miracles for many years. In 2002, she finally accepted Jesus Christ as her Lord and Savior. She thanks God daily for His abundant love and mercy.